Taf'
116
San A

Time to face the music.

Jacob's Body

John Bankston
Book Two in The Academy Series

Mitchell Lane

PUBLISHERS

2001 SW 31st Avenue
Hallandale, FL 33009
www.mitchelllane.com

Copyright © 2024 by Mitchell Lane Publishers. All rights reserved. No part of this book may be reproduced without written permission from the publisher. Printed and bound in the United States of America.

First Edition, 2024.

Author: John Bankston
Designer: Ed Morgan

Title: The Academy: Jacob's Body
Description: Hallandale, FL : Mitchell Lane Publishers, [2024]

Library bound ISBN: 978-1-68020-847-4
eBook ISBN: 978-1-68020-850-4

… I came to myself, in a dark wood, where the direct way was lost. It is a hard thing to speak of, how wild, harsh and impenetrable that wood was, so that thinking of it recreates the fear. It is scarcely less bitter than death: but, in order to tell of the good that I found there, I must tell of the other things I saw there.

–Inferno Canto I: 1-60 The Dark Wood and the Hill
Dante: The Divine Comedy

INTRO

You didn't think it was possible to dream of nothing until you did.
The memory haunted you for days, remembered in a way few dreams are.
There was no light, no sound. No sight.
There was only the darkness—darkness and a growing sense that you will never get out.
And in your waking moments of clarity the questions:
Who put you here?
And why?

CHAPTER ONE
Friday
November 11th

The corpse swung from the ceiling, skin fraying around the blood-soaked rope, black tongue lolling, bulging eyes staring straight into mine. I screamed as the basement walls shook and the filing cabinets rattled below.

"*No! No! No!*" a boy's voice carried over the din. I turned to run up the rest of the stairs, and there he stood, so close we could have touched—if he'd been real. My flashlight's beam cut through him. I stumbled backward, grabbing the railing. My light winked out. When it came back on, Jacob was gone.

I didn't want to look behind me. I still did. The corpse rocked like a pendulum, the old iron pipe creaking from the weight. *Jacob's father.*

He'd been dead for over 20 years.

Dust rained down on me. My hip slammed against the doorknob. Jacob's father raised an almost skeletal arm and pointed to the lock. The door popped open like a cork from a champagne bottle.

Across the cabin's dusty living room, discarded desks formed ghostly silhouettes. When I'd arrived, I'd stepped as lightly as a ballerina. Leaving, my feet pounded the floorboards, crunching glass from the shattered windowpane. Despite the air billowing through, the room stank of must and decay.

Now, even after escaping the cabin, I'm still trapped. Because if I focus on my audition, someone I care about will die. If I blow off practice and focus on finding her, I could be killed.

THE ACADEMY

Sheila. The reason I broke into the cabin today. The reason I'm risking expulsion and maybe my life. She is a violin prodigy who spent the fall prepping me for a cello audition, my last chance at redemption after a year of screw-ups. One week ago, she left just before dinner and never returned. Her things were removed from our dorm room. The next day, I took a bus to her parents' place in Stowe to find her.

I don't care what the headmaster told our housemother. Sheila *wasn't* in Stowe, and she hadn't been there in weeks. Other than cleaners, I doubt anyone had been there since our failed ski trip, when Sheila had run off with some random dude and left me alone to wallow in wine and self-pity. This time there was no luggage, nothing to indicate Sheila was planning a trip. Her current passport was still tucked away in a dresser drawer. That's why I think Collins is lying. I don't know what Sheila is doing, but I know she isn't in Stowe and she isn't helping her parents teach music in some rural village in China.

She's not the first teenager to go missing from our school. That would be Jacob. The cabin, my dorm—all the land and most of the buildings that became The Northeast Kingdom Academy of Music & Art—had belonged to Jacob's family. After the sale, his father hanged himself and Jacob disappeared.

In the last week, I've seen them both.

There've been other missing students over the last twenty years. Sheila had left a clue about Amber in a journal she'd hid in our practice room. In the photo with the article about her disappearance, Amber looked like me. She even played the cello. Ten years ago, Amber was missing for exactly two weeks. Then they found her body. Sherman at the bookstore told me she'd been kept alive until the very end.

If that same sick killer had Sheila, there was only one week left before he killed her too.

One week.

One week to figure all this out. One week to find Jacob's body and connect Headmaster Collins to his death. And, oh yeah. One week before my last shot at my first-choice school. Next Friday I'll be in New York, auditioning with the composition Sheila taught me. If I slack off, Collins will know. And he's the last person in the world I want to make suspicious.

CHAPTER TWO

The driveway from the Academy exits at the crest of a huge hill. To the right, the road slopes toward the nearest town. I race along the edge in the opposite direction, my knapsack burdened with the weight of Jacob's file. If I'm fast enough, I can catch the headmaster with grimy hands like mine—proof that he locked me in the basement. I'm no longer scared.

I'm angry.

Darlene told me about the cabin. She thinks I'm wrong about Sheila, wrong about Collins. She still helped me. Even loaned me the unreliable flashlight.

The cabin is one mile from our dorm and Darlene uses it as a marker when she runs. During a recent downpour, she'd sought shelter on the porch. Peering through the windows, she noticed filing cabinets in the living room. It wasn't on school grounds, she told me, but it was clearly Academy property.

I'd broken in hoping for answers. The oldest files were secreted in the basement. The Academy's first class numbered just a dozen, Jacob among them. His file was twice as thick as the rest. Before I could peek inside, the lights went out and my flashlight stopped working. Through the doorway, I saw a man's hand. Across his wrist lay a splash of purple ink.

Then the door had slammed shut. I'd heard it being locked; a moment later, footsteps. The basement's windows were too narrow to slide through, but I could have escaped by breaking down the door.

JACOB'S BODY

Which means whoever locked me in didn't want to kill me. They wanted to slow me down.

It worked—until the shades of Jacob and his father lit a fire under my feet.

Instead of crossing the street to my dorm, I head toward the Headmaster's Residence. More hotel than home, it's usually occupied by touring musicians, connected parents, elderly donors. Collins keeps the upstairs rooms full of guests, while the downstairs is devoted to fundraisers and concerts.

Passing the valet stand, I don't hesitate at the steps. Taking them two at a time, I slip past the open door and cross the foyer. A table has been set up for an impromptu coat check. Behind it a bored girl reads a paperback, making easy cash. Sheila told me Darlene does these sorts of gigs all the time.

The last time I came here was in September. I was newly transferred. My best outfits are in a closet back at my mother's Cambridge condo. I'd assumed they wouldn't get much wear at a northern Vermont school closer to Canada than a decent symphony. At five feet and 100 pounds, Sheila could have maybe lent me a scarf. I'd settled for a sweater too warm for early fall and slacks that needed an iron. It was fancied up with jewelry I'd untangled. When we arrived at the headmaster's, I wondered why I'd bothered.

Acting as tour guide, Sheila led us to a space that reminded me of a ballroom in some old painting. Enormous chandeliers sparkled overhead. The vast oak floor was dotted with narrow buffet tables. At the far end, a string quartet performed next to a roped-off dance floor. I heard the accents of home, of Boston and

THE ACADEMY

New York, where Sheila had spent her reckless early teens. When I traced the sounds to their speakers, I saw elderly couples who'd adopted their new state's style: flannel shirts, faded jeans, practical boots. My dorm mate was ready for the Met Ball in a shimmering red gown that emphasized her tan shoulders and perfect up-do. As usual, she bridged height differences with stilettos.

Sheila usually headlined concerts and displayed her framed posters to prove it. But before she came to The Academy, she'd endured rumors of scandal supported by suggestive, unfocused pictures on gossip sites. Instead of cowering, she owned every room she entered. At the headmaster's, she'd stood out. She spoke with the diction of a well-educated socialite. When she smiled or touched your arm, you felt like she cared about you above all others. When she left my side, I tracked her blond hair across the room. She was my safe harbor whenever I got sick of grown-ups memorializing my father.

Julius Barnes was a Grammy-winning cellist. To me, he was just Dad. He'd always made time to help with a composition or a homework problem—even from four thousand miles away. What stands out about that night at the headmaster's are my father's acquaintances mumbling condolences or stumbling over apologies for missing his memorial.

I chafed at the requirement to be gracious, to be considerate. Listening to people who barely knew my dad acting like they knew everything about him makes me want to scream.

Not cry. The tears dried up a long time ago.

Inevitably, someone always mentions how empty the music world was without him. What about my world? What about my emptiness? Every time I played the cello, it reminded me of what I'd lost. Sheila helped me rediscover my love for the instrument.

Now she's gone. Just like my dad.

CHAPTER THREE

Inside the Headmaster's Residence, I shake off the memories and squint down the hallway that stretches past the foyer. The lights are dim and far apart, inviting shadows. I wonder if Jacob has been here, before or after he died. Then I remember. Like most of the campus buildings that look antique, this one went up in the last ten years.

The walls are lined with black-and-white photographs. They show various Academy events, graduating classes, perfect landscapes. Every one of them was taken this century. By New England boarding school standards, it's a tiny blip of time. Yet they look like they were created when cameras required tripods and huge flashes. For some reason, this creeps me out even more than the shadows.

The great room's doors are open. It smells of lilacs, but there aren't any fresh flowers. Something about the space begs for reverent silence.

Opposite the entrance, a small stage has been erected. Like last time, four chairs and four music stands await a string quartet. Now though, instead of banquet tables and a dance area, small round tables are spaced neatly across the floor. Ironed linen tablecloths are spread over them, waiting for place settings.

"Are you joining us tonight?"

I don't turn but every muscle in my body tightens. It's who I came to see. *Headmaster Collins*. I imagine him as he would appear after locking me in the basement. I picture his hands darkened with grime from the cabin, his pant legs muddy from the driveway.

Instead, he's as elegant as any man I've known. He's good-looking for his age, with a smooth forehead and thick black hair. His cap-toed patent leather shoes shine to reflection; his tuxedo looks sewn for him. His wrists are graced by French cuffs. He could have locked me in the basement with enough time to get ready, but it seems unfathomable. I've never seen him flustered, and now his calm is familiar. For once, his smile meets his eyes.

We'd met last April, during the time of year locals call "Mud Season." Late snow was already melting but the cold nights held little promise of spring. He gave a private tour to my mother and me, discussing the shinier bits of Academy history along with anecdotes about successful grads. We'd flown from Boston to Burlington, although driving would have been faster. My mother refused to get behind the wheel after my father's accident, and I'd never gotten around to earning my license.

"Casey?"

"I'm not ready." My voice is a squeak. I cough to bring it up a register.

"No, no, not to perform. Just to watch. It might be a nice distraction from audition prep."

I start at this, trying to detect sarcasm. After the campus tour, my mother was enthusiastic. Manhattan Conservatory had just rejected me. She held my previous school responsible for my bad behavior. I knew better, of course, but I also knew that there was no getting out of this forced transfer. Collins had relaxed the requirements for senior transfers in my favor, and then put me with Sheila the Star.

On our return flight, my mother complimented Collins' youthful good looks and sharp eye for talent. I'd noticed something else. It was the way he gazed at me when he thought no one else was looking. It wasn't a leer. It was pity. I could tell he expected even less of me than I did of myself. If I succeeded, if I got into the Conservatory on my second try, the program he'd founded would get all the credit. If I failed again, everyone would assume it was because I was too damaged to take advantage of all the Academy offered, to alter the dark trajectory of my life.

Before Sheila disappeared, Collins barely spoke to me. This week, he's everywhere— pushing me to practice, pushing me to focus. Maybe I'm wrong but I don't think it's about encouraging me. I think he wants to make sure I'm not busy looking for Sheila. I'm worried about how much he knows or thinks he knows about what I've been doing.

Until today my investigation into missing teenagers yielded little more than an on-campus restriction. Yesterday he'd expressed disappointment at how I was wasting my cello teacher's valuable time after I'd skipped a private to visit the town newspaper and Elba's Books. Thinking about this helps me craft a quick lie. "Actually I was trying to find Mr. Keifer. I think he mentioned being here."

Which is stupid, he avoids these things like deer ticks. Collins says as much: "Doug? Are they offering skating lessons in hell?"

I laugh harder than I should, nervously giggling over his weak profanity. "You're right, I must have gotten confused."

He smiles even more broadly. "What is it you're always saying? 'No worries'? Seriously Casey, if you can tear yourself away from the cello, come by later. Dinner isn't served until eight—gives you some time to clean up."

I start at this, but then nod and head out the way I came in. A mirror stops me.

I suddenly realize why Collins didn't say "get ready" or "put on something fancy." He said, "clean up." My rotation of worn jeans and dark shirts will never land me on a best-dressed listicle but the reflection reveals tracks of dust across my face. I'd had my hair in a ponytail, but the band broke. Now it's a brown tangle that falls over my sharp cheekbones and high forehead. I struggle to remove an errant twig currently substituting as an accessory. I rip a few strands out as well. There's a fresh tear across the knee of my jeans, revealing a small patch of dried blood on my skin.

Exiting, I recognize my boot tracks on an otherwise clean carpet. Then I notice something else. Faded footprints run parallel to my own, then veer toward the stairs. They are bigger than mine, with the grooves of a boot rather than the smooth sole of a dress shoe. I follow them, peering up the steps to the second floor.

The muddy prints are the same color as the cabin's drive—not like the muck on campus. I'm certain they belong to whoever locked me in the basement. Could it have been Collins after all? I remember suddenly that I never heard a car. The person who trapped me either parked nearer the road or walked. Which would have taken time—time he couldn't have had.

Did he have help?

I'm about to sneak upstairs when I hear voices near the entrance. Not wanting to get caught, I slink outside, looking better suited for a field party than a four-course meal with student accompaniment.

THE ACADEMY

Watching the first arrivals hand over their keys to attendants, I think about an earlier party. It was the night before my Conservatory audition.

CHAPTER FOUR

One single bad decision isn't why I transferred to The Academy. I'd made a long string of bad decisions in the weeks after my father's death. It was the last one, the fate-sealing choice I'm still paying for.

It was a party. That's all.

It was identical to the dozens of others I'd attended in the restless, blurry haze of junior year. I'd been going to them long before people started excusing them as my way of grieving. Except this Friday was different.

The next morning, I'd be auditioning for a fall spot at the Manhattan Conservatory.

I should have ignored the texts, but by nine o'clock, I could no longer endure my mother's need to fill silence with questions. My room's dim solitude seemed too bleak. I called Christopher. He believed me when I said getting my mind off everything was just what I needed.

When I arrived, college kids were shoulder to shoulder—some of them hip to hip, grinding to Parisian trance. My dead father wasn't movie-star famous, but within that rundown house on Cambridge's seedy fringes, I was a celebutant (or celebutard).

Introductions flowed as quickly as drinks.

I kept Christopher's thin cashmere sweater in a death grip as we waded past glued-together couples and floating party orphans. Sipping and gulping toward warm forgetfulness, I was grateful for my boyfriend's quiet understanding.

The living room was too crowded with fragrant smoke and excited conversations, the kitchen dominated by boozers too much like mirrors. We cuddled in the untended backyard as biting wind whipped in from the Charles.

Our kisses tasted like rum and cigarettes: sweet and bitter.

Then there's a memory hole.

The bedroom is the next thing I remember. Somehow I was sober enough to be silly. If I'd seemed drunk or sad, Christopher wouldn't have given in.

I'll always regret most of that night. But I'll never regret the interlude we shared atop a blanket of discarded coats. Christopher had hoped for a perfect moment.

Perfect moments are fairy tales.

I remember getting up and locking the door. My boyfriend remained immobile across a faded comforter. Turning slowly toward him, I began adding my clothing to the down jackets and vintage trench coats. Buzzed and bold, I got naked without turning off the light, enjoying his gaze.

I constructed a small hill of borrowed sweater, overpriced jeans, Target t-shirt. I turned toward the door before adding my bra and underwear, tossing them behind me with a flourish.

I spun and the room did the same. Catching my breath, I told him nothing would change.

It wasn't the first time I'd lied to him. It was the first time I believed my fiction.

After that, memory is less movie than photographs. Those images are accompanied by a background noise more like a hum than a moan that could have come only from my lips.

It took longer than I'd thought it would. If there was any pain, it was subsumed by more persistent hurts.

The next day I awoke sore and still a little drunk. I'm not sure why I even bothered going to the audition.

CHAPTER FIVE

Just past the Headmaster's Residence, students are queuing up outside the dining hall. When Jacob attended, the dining hall was still a barn. I think about going in and looking for Darlene. It's too much to handle. Besides looking like I spent the day digging mushrooms, I'm carrying stolen school property inside my knapsack.

As I cross the street toward my dorm. I think about the party, about the failed audition, about The Academy. I think about the cabin and the ghost of Jacob's father—and how he saved me.

I'd like to be able to save myself.

But I can't keep doing this alone.

My dad died. And I couldn't manage my audition.

Sheila is gone. And I'm wrecking my second chance.

If I had convinced Darlene to come with me, maybe she would have seen what I saw. When I'd asked, she'd reminded me she was on scholarship and couldn't afford to get caught. If instead of locking me in the basement the intruder had turned me in, Collins would have made one phone call and my second Manhattan C audition would have had the same result as my first.

At Dorm A's front porch, I lean against the railing.

Everything shifts.

My inner monologue is replaced by a boy's voice. It's familiar. I heard it in August, in dreams without context. I heard it at the cabin. It's Jacob's. He calls his dad "Pa." Father and son had their own name for my dorm: "Our New Place." It was christened when Jacob's mother was alive, before cancer consumed her and the family's dreams. Before Pa drank away their property, practically gifting fallow fields and run-down buildings to a conductor in his late 20s with dreams of his own.

I see my dorm as it was long ago—skirted with scaffolding and boasting fresh paint. It shimmers in the bright light of August. I swelter beneath late-afternoon, late-summer sunshine. My third-floor room is directly overhead. It's part of the original building—the foundation was poured in 1865.

The hallucination is augmented. When I see Collins, he looks younger than my housemom, sporting tousled hair like he's in a boy band. He'd be pretty if it weren't for the gun.

The person he's aiming at materializes: Jacob. I understand instinctively that this is what happened after he found his father. Collins must have been lying in wait at the cabin.

Collins gives Jacob a brutal shove. The ghost boy stumbles through the doorway. I only see his face for a single, fleeting second. His eyes are half shut. He isn't screaming; he isn't fighting back. His battle was earlier, referenced by the fresh bruise marring the headmaster's cheek.

Sunlight disappears in an instant. I'm cold.

I've never seen Jacob inside my dorm. Is his body here, beneath concrete and carpeting? If Collins killed him here, wouldn't the boy also be haunting my room or the hallways?

"Oh my God, perfect timing! Do I have a surprise for you!"

I jump, more startled by the voice than I was by the apparition.

"Our New Place" is my dorm once again, the open front door familiar. Darlene is leaning out, barefoot, in loose jeans and a huge hoodie. I discovered recently that her baggy clothes cover a buff body but haven't figured out why she conceals what she's worked so hard to achieve.

"What's up?"

Instead of answering, she steps back. Her dark hair is damp, like she's just stepped out of the shower. I smell something like perfume as I slip past. Her eyes are twinkling. She's 15 but looks more like a little kid on Christmas morning. Before I'd been ready to tell her what happened at the cabin. Now I'm too confused to say hello.

When Sheila was here, Darlene barely spoke. Now she's a little chatterbox, giggly and girlish—as if her shyness disappeared along with my dorm mate.

I suspect Darlene wants to show me something in her room, but instead of continuing down the first-floor hallway, she veers to the right. Past our lobby, stairs lead to the basement. These steps are carpeted, the room recently updated. Its subterranean aspect still recalls where I was imprisoned.

I am *so* done with basements. A hard pledge to keep in New England, where every other teenager boasts a remodeled belowground lair with flat screens and hidden booze.

Our dorm offers a laundry facility and study area, but it's also the only one with a music room. It even has two pianos. Before we turn the corner, I recognize Emily's sure-fingered Mahler. She lives across the way, in newly built housing with its own kitchen and actual boys, but what it lacks is a piano. Hers has an artist space. Not sure how The Academy determined room assignments. I'd say chance or a lottery, but I know Sheila requested me.

And then I get it. *Sheila.* Sheila must be down here! And Emily is playing her audition piece for her. I'm debating between hiking cross-campus to retrieve my cello from the music building or settling for the well-worn model leaning against the wall. I want Sheila to know I didn't slack off during her missing week—almost as much as I want to hear her guaranteed to be mind-blowing explanation for why she disappeared. And where did she go?

I'm thinking all of this when Emily stops playing. The light atop the piano illuminates white keys and her bright red shoulder-length hair. It does not dispel the shadows. A boy rises from the couch. I step back, startled by Jacob's appearance after being so convinced he wouldn't be here.

Then another familiar voice calls my name.

I'm trying to hide my disappointment when Christopher gives me a hug.

CHAPTER SIX

I don't speak. I drink Christopher in. His light brown hair has gotten shaggier since FaceTiming in September. He's sporting stubble. In the glow from the piano light, his blue eyes twinkle.

I press my face to his coat, which is new and soft and absorbs my tears. His gentle fingers find a gap beneath my jacket and travel upward, tracing a line below my ribs.

"There's no school because of the holiday, so I decided to take a drive," he says, his voice muffled because I'm still pressed against him. "I hope you don't mind the surprise."

I step back, putting my face against my sleeve. When I look at him, my eyes are clear. "No, not even a little."

Emily has stopped playing. Darlene stares at us. They barely exist.

"This is the best surprise ever." For a second, there is the flash of uglier surprises—like the one haunting that underground warren of boxes and files, like the specters I saw on the porch. "Did you…" My voice hiccups and I swallow the words.

Instead I collapse on the sofa, grateful for dim lighting. My hands are scratched, my nails filthy. I slip them under my thighs while a worried look travels across Darlene's face.

"Are you okay, Casey?" That awful, familiar question is only tolerable from his lips. My hands tremble beneath my jeans. Until my party recollection earlier, I've barely thought of him. Now, Christopher is quickly crowding out everything else.

Which is exactly what I need.

He sits beside me, his manicured nails shiny as he strokes my leg. I put my hand over his, dirty skin covering clean. "Did you come all the way up here for me?"

"Of course. Why else would I be here?"

"I hear Killington might get fresh powder this weekend."

He laughs loudly at our inside joke. Christopher started composing around the time he was reading *Goodnight Moon*. Growing up, his parents were more likely to let him play drinking games with a buzzsaw than give him permission to snowboard. Now that's he's almost an adult, they're actually more intrusive.

As if reading my mind, he says, "I needed a break. Senior year should be a goof, but it's been nothing but demos and meetings and arguments. My parents don't get that I'd rather be the next Zedd than the next Van Cliburn."

It would help if I could sympathize. Like Sheila, Christopher had an easy time getting into his first-choice school. He's also just as likely to spend his college years on some sort of global tour.

He misreads my silence. "Hey, I'm sorry for just showing up like this. I know you have the audition next week. I don't want to get in the way."

"It's fine. Believe it or not, I've been working pretty hard at it since Sheila left."

"Wait. Sheila's gone?"

"Long story." Wow, just when I think I'm used to the Dark Ages, I'm reminded of what a pain communicating from here can be. I haven't even emailed him from the library. Most boyfriends would be pissed but he's more focused on music than anyone I know—and I know a bushel of OCD prodigies. I'm sure he's glad I'm finally spending time on what matters.

If he only knew.

"I should have called," he says. I smile at the absurdity of him trying to get me on the dorm's house phone.

I stand so quickly my head spins. Leaning against the back of the couch, I ask, "Can we get out of here?"

Christopher nods. "Sure. Of course. Do you need to go upstairs or..."

Leaning over, I kiss him on the cheek. "Just give me a bit, okay?"

He nods, smiling, as he reaches for a discarded newspaper. He examines it like an archeologist. Emily starts playing a ballad I don't recognize. I think she wrote it. Darlene is on the other couch pretending to read her romance when she's really memorizing mine.

I don't blame her.

It's early evening at the start of a holiday weekend but the dorm is deathly quiet. I'd expected laughter, plans shouted up the stairway. Instead, I don't see anyone as I ascend toward my floor. Most of the younger girls are probably off on ski vacations or other diversions; many of the older ones are preparing for auditions that are right around the corner. It's where I should be—instead of spending time with a dropping-in boyfriend or chasing phantoms.

Phantoms. This is what I'm thinking while light shifts from twilight in the shadowy hallway. The word follows me into the clutter of my room.

I was set back on my heels when I realized it was Christopher and not Sheila waiting for me. Now, I'm faintly giddy with anticipation. We haven't had a proper date in months. I actually start humming as I pick up discarded socks and put them in the hamper; recover a B-minus test paper scattered by my bureau. The bed is as I left it: a twisted tangle of sheets and sleeping bag-comforter. There's no way I'm sneaking my boy up here—it's way too risky. Yet still I make my bed, spreading the bag so the interior plaid faces the ceiling. Sheila once joked it makes me look like a hobo intern, but at least it's warm.

Glancing out the window, I realize the sun has set completely and the streetlights are on. It's a habit now—staring at the walkway in front of Dorm A, expecting to see Sheila or even Jacob. Tonight there is no one. Turning back, I realize my overhead isn't bright enough to dispel all the shadows. I conjure all manner of uglies in the corners. Grabbing my towel and shower caddy, I leave the door open as I race from the room.

CHAPTER SEVEN

I've lived on campus for three months. I doubt I'll ever get used to sharing a bathroom. It's not like the ones at health clubs or schools. The toilets are enclosed by actual walls and doors; the showers are in stalls with curtains separating them from private changing areas. Only the sinks are in the open, two rows of them stretching beneath tall mirrors. One row faces the toilets, the other the showers. Weekday mornings and weekend nights, a line forms for the facilities.

Right now is prime time, but when I open the door the room is as vacant as the stairs and the hallway. For the first time in a while, I wish I had company.

A couple of minutes later, I'm letting the shower warm up while peeling off my clothes beside a bench. I'm disgusted by how much dirt and dried mud is cascading onto the floor. I wish I'd done this in the room, where the dirt wouldn't turn back into mud. As I sweep some of it to the edge with my heel, I notice a dark line just above my ankles where socks and jeans didn't meet.

Ducking into the spray, I flinch as it hits the cuts and scrapes on my knees and arms. A perfect, knob-shaped circle is tattooed on my hip—it's shifting from red to purple. The water swirling around my toes is brown at first, then clear.

Sometimes I envy short-haired girls and moms who hack off their tresses in the name of convenience. But my long hair is one of my best features, the last thing about myself I stopped caring about. Tonight it's a serious mess, yielding another branch and a few leaves as I run my fingers through it. It takes a long time to wash, just as it always takes a long time to dry. I add a huge glob of conditioner and hope for the best.

Long hair, of course, is what I think about when I think about Sheila. Her blond locks stood out in real life and on concert posters. They differentiated her from dark-haired musicians, gave a California vibe to a New York girl. Her locks are why I'm certain she isn't strolling around campus—because even more than her attitude, her hair stood out from 100 yards away.

As the water massages my bruised skin, my thoughts drift from my missing dorm mate. Christopher's arrival really was perfect timing, an ideal interlude. Since I got here, he has never been far from my thoughts. My heart already ached from my father's death; saying goodbye to my boyfriend was agony. When I wasn't waking up from nightmares, I was waking with his name on my lips, sweat prickling my neck. The long hours of practice were a relief, focusing on something other than what was no longer an arm's length away. Yet it was only after Sheila vanished that I stopped thinking about him completely. Saving Sheila has been all-consuming.

The guilt fades as washing myself fresh and clean suddenly feels uplifting, *powerful*. A fizzy feeling starts just below my belly button—like an ice-cold can of soda popped on a hot day. The water feels different, too, caressing instead of stinging. When it hits my skin, every sensation is heightened. A tingle travels up my spine and the inside of my thighs. A hot flush blooms across my chest and throat.

Knowing Christopher is just three floors below me instead of hours away only increases everything. A sigh escapes my lips as I close my eyes.

The curtain rustles.

I freeze, blinking and peering through the steam toward the door. I try to hear footsteps or flushing over the sound of the shower—assuming another girl has entered and she's let in a draft. Turning away from the curtain, I see a shadow.

Jacob leans against the shower wall.

I'm mortified and horrified: broiling from embarrassment, shivering from fear. If he were a living, breathing human being he would be soaked. Yet instead of drenching his clothes or piercing his ghostly skin, the water stops a few inches from his body. It's a force field, a thin line between his glowing white T-shirt and the spray.

I have one arm across my chest, the other extended straight down in an attempt to cover up. His eyes are unwavering, focused only on my own. He doesn't glance down, not even for a second. As much as I want to turn and run, I remain where I am, with the cold curtain against my hip.

I wait for him to speak, for him to explain why he chose this of all times and places to materialize. Then I remember my vision from earlier—Collins marching him past the scaffolding and through the threshold of what would become this dorm. I saw enough to guess that Jacob was most likely killed here, but as I meet his steady gaze, I become certain of it.

He doesn't speak.

I reach over and turn off the shower, feeling less modest by the second. I stand there in the steam inches from a ghost as humiliation is replaced by another emotion. It's definitely not fear.

Exiting, I don't reach for the towel.

I turn, hoping to see him looking at me. Instead, he's shrinking. I gasp. Only then do I realize he's slipping through the floor, his eyes shut, his face in agony.

I know what I have to do. I hope Christopher isn't too married to any date plans. Because in order to find Jacob's body, I'm going to need his help.

CHAPTER EIGHT

Instead of being concerned about the distraction of my plus-one, Collins pulls Christopher to the side a minute after my introduction. This is what I was counting on. The headmaster already knew who Christopher was, of course. I doubt there's anyone who runs a music school who hasn't heard of him. He's my polar opposite: top grades, early acceptances, planned tours, record deal. It's crazy he loves me in spite of the things that make me a less than ideal student. *Or a less than an ideal girlfriend.*

Collins is such a star-effer that he can't wait to share his experiences contributing to that Guetta track. When he asks Christopher's opinion about some obscure French DJ, slipping away unnoticed isn't even a challenge.

This wasn't my boyfriend's dream date night. It's just Collins' invitation actually sounded sincere. Christopher knows how much I've struggled, how much I need to stay (or get into) the Headmaster's good graces. It was actually fun picking out an outfit, even if my black cashmere sweater and dark slacks look more cat burglar than concert goer. Thank God it's cold enough that I can choose things out of my dresser drawers, that I no longer regret abandoning dresses in Cambridge. Brightened by a thin silver chain from my dad and the Buffalo Exchange leather jacket, it looks acceptable.

Christopher, of course, always looks acceptable.

The room is packed. I dodge uniformed servers and flanneled aficionados. I see a Mostly Mozart star in a tuxedo and a young recording artist in pink overalls. I offer quick hellos to the few who recognize me while trying not to think too much about my father's memorial.

THE ACADEMY

Unlike a few hours ago, this time I have a plan.

Racing here after escaping the cabin, I'd hoped to catch Collins red-handed. I'd expected him to bear traces of mud from the driveway, to be out of breath and nervous. I have no idea what I would have done if he'd matched my imagination. Beat a confession out of him? Call the cops? If he's really responsible for a bunch of dead and missing teenagers, I doubt things would have gone all that well.

I'm not sure where Sheila is, if she's hidden in one of the campus buildings or miles away. I believe with all my hope and heart that she's alive. She probably wasn't here when I arrived earlier, probably wasn't bound and gagged in a spare room or trapped in the basement below the ballroom. Yet if Collins is involved, there has to be a clue somewhere in this building.

The outer doors are propped open as guests continue arriving, bringing with them bursts of cold air and expensive cologne. Peering past the threshold, I see valets spiriting away older Subarus and Volvos.

A narrow hallway stretches opposite the ballroom, beginning past the foyer. Halfway down, back stairs lead to the second floor. This is where Collins lives, alongside honored guests enjoying accommodations as well appointed as five-star hotel suites. It would be too easy to get caught poking around up there by some genius musician taking a break from squeezing flesh with donors. Besides, I really don't think there's anything to find; it's too in the middle of everything.

I wind my way past occupied bathrooms and random rooms with open doors. There's an office, but it's almost barren. It's probably intended for guests; the headmaster's is in Admin. At the hallway's dead end, I encounter a room with a closed door.

After checking to make sure no one is watching, I turn the knob. It's unlocked.

The hallway light barely reaches past the doorway. Despite the scary shadows, I slip in quickly and shut the door behind me. The switch is to the side; mercifully it turns on the overhead when I touch it.

The room looks like it holds everything that might get used in the ballroom. There are boxes of napkins and packing paper covering plates and bowls. Glassware has been piled haphazardly in one corner; linens are stacked in another. It reminds me of the cabin, which sends a tight knot into my stomach.

I exhale slowly as I move around a crate that's almost as tall as I am. Behind it, I see a familiar set of Tumi luggage. This is what had occupied half our closet. Leaning over, I see a tag with Sheila's name and her New York address printed out in neat handwriting. I grab the handle of the suitcase and lift. It's heavy, stuffed no doubt with everything that could be squeezed in. Her garment bag is distended, looking like a sausage casing filled to bursting. Not everything fit, evidently, because some of her dresses are dumped nearby. The ones on top are wrinkled and stained. They look like they were tossed into the back of a grimy truck. I'd assumed when Darlene told me some guys packed up Sheila's half of our room that they were professionals. I imagined the careful men my mother or my dorm mate's parents would have hired. I feel myself inexplicably wanting to cry. Sheila had such pretty things. They were obviously brought here by men Collins hired on the cheap, selected for their speed and not their skill.

Beside the dresses are her shoeboxes. Sheila revered her shoes, each pair removed and returned with the care you'd give a family heirloom. There is a single open cardboard box, maybe two feet tall and crammed with textbooks and binders. There is little point digging through it. The headmaster must have looked everywhere for Sheila's journal before asking me about it.

Except there are few other options and I don't feel like opening her luggage.

I sit down on the floor and take everything out of the box. Then I slowly flip through each item before returning it. There are notebooks where every page is filled and dog-eared magazines about teen celebrities. There are textbooks so new the binding pops when I open them and biographies she got secondhand at The Strand. I'm almost done when a well-folded paper covered with blue ink flutters to the floor.

I open it. It's a blueprint for my dorm—plans dated 25 years ago. This is when it was being remodeled, the year Jacob and his father died. On the basement level, I see markings for the music area and the sitting area and the new stairs. At the far end, someone has used a red pen to draw a square. I turn the page this way and that.

The laundry room. I'm sure of it.

I refold the blueprint and slip it into my purse.

Standing up, I make sure everything else is back in place. That's when I see a group of boxes I didn't notice earlier. I walk over, assuming the labels are meaningless, that someone used them to pack books or plates because they are sturdy. My mouth waters when I realize the boxes are still factory sealed. The sound of the top giving way to my desperation is so loud I assume it can be heard in the foyer.

JACOB'S BODY

I don't care. I've found the bar's extra storage, and I have a water bottle in my purse.

CHAPTER NINE

At the last minute, I decide to leave some water in the bottle. I'll think about this later with something like pride. The container is small, sure, but I still remember eighth grade health class. One ounce of liquor equals a standard drink. The bottle is 12 ounces. *Twelve drinks.* With the water, it's maybe seven.

I down some in the storage room and enjoy a few secretive sips in a bathroom. Back in the ballroom, I'm relaxed and giddy all at once. I feel sorry for teens who'll never experience the unique joy of being loaded with a live string quartet accompaniment. Mozart and Brahms and random contemporary covers cascade over me. Despite Collin's admiration for Christopher, we're seated at a far back table. I slip my hand beneath the linen cloth and put it high up on his thigh. He doesn't stop me, doesn't seem to notice that I'm buzzed.

In spite of everything, the thought that this is low-key behavior for me makes me a little bit sad. Not sad enough to slow down, but still…

Later, I even eat—enjoying the roast chicken with almost the same pleasure as I enjoyed the music. We slip out during a speech, Christopher shivering despite his coat. "It seems colder here."

"Than Boston? Christopher, compared to here, Boston is Florida." I pirouette slowly across the street, feeling warmer than I have in weeks. I spot his green Range Rover. If I'd come from the music building instead of the woods, I would have passed it on my way to the dorm.

JACOB'S BODY

It's not curfew yet. He waits while I run in, tripping up the stairs but somehow avoiding Winter and her scrutiny, Darlene and her salacious curiosity. The building is still eerily quiet as I retrieve my knapsack. When I return, he takes it and puts it on the back seat beside my purse. Then he opens the door and helps me up, leaving me to fumble with the seatbelt.

I watch The Academy diminish in my mirror. Soon, the Rover's headlights discover the gap in the woods. I peer up the overgrown drive leading to the cabin. An indistinct shape is barely visible through the trees. It's a vehicle, its brights aimed toward the porch.

I rest my hand on Christopher's knee, grateful for warm connection. It can't be Collins; I just saw him. My curiosity is so strong it's all I can do not to beg my boyfriend to stop.

Instead, we barrel toward town.

Just like Emily a few days ago, he's forced to hit his brakes as the town's one light blinks from yellow to red. The last time, I'd seen a girl in the crosswalk. Her hair was streaked with blue, her legs white and bare beneath an A-line dress that barely moved despite the wind. She'd been wearing combat boots. The light turned green and Emily darted forward, the girl dissipating like fog.

There's no sign of her this time.

There's also no traffic, no reason for us to be stopped. The car is almost silent, just the muffled hum of the engine. I'm squeezing Christopher's leg. Before he can say anything, I shift away to turn on the radio. A college station out of Bennington is playing the kind of music he likes. Turning it up kills his questions. Maybe, just maybe, it will also keep the ghosts at bay.

THE ACADEMY

A few minutes later, we reach downtown. I imagine the landscape through Christopher's eyes. Main Street boasts swaybacked structures, slow-shuffling locals, and an out-of-service service station. The tiny curio shop's display window seems more tacky than kitsch. Desperate for money from out-of-staters, its glass is sheathed with "For Sale" and "Discount" come-ons. All of it is familiar now, almost like home.

My posher Boston friends are always seeking out vintage diners in undiscovered neighborhoods, but Christopher drives right past Al's. I'm about to ask where he's going when he brakes at the entrance to The Waverly Inn. I keep quiet as he maneuvers up the gentle hill, the drive lined by miniature pines covered in lights and faux snow.

Most Academy kids only eat here when their parents visit. Plus, I had more than my daily allotment of food at the headmaster's.

His voice is throaty when he says, "I really missed you."

I lean toward him, kissing him with naked lips. My belly grows warm as I realize we're not here for a meal. Missing curfew is no longer a concern. Because after all I've gone through today and the many, many ways my mind has tortured me all week, I know one sure way of forgetting everything.

CHAPTER TEN
Saturday
November 12th

In the darkness, there is only kissing. The singular contact of our lips. My first connection in days, weeks... months.

His fingertips discover the bare skin of my lower back. As they do, my darker thoughts unspool in threads of purple and white. Behind my eyelids, colors flash like tracers. His touch is cool, cold even, but I don't complain. For I am burning hot, molten. My entire body feels poised on the precipice of an active volcano. Lava bubbles in my capillaries.

Closer.

More contact points, more places for skin to connect with skin. Sighs are created in my belly, nurtured in my heart, born from my lips. My arms wrap around him. My breath lingers across his ear.

I open my eyes.

Jacob kisses my neck.

I start awake with the sensation of falling. Beside me, Christopher doesn't even stir.

Blinking, the last moments of the dream slide off me like a membrane. Diffused light falls through thick curtains, staining the room orange. Barely revealed are two chairs upholstered in matching damask, the mahogany credenza that hides the flat-screen.

I remain immobile. The bed my last link to bliss. I want to remain forever beneath high-thread-count sheets atop the four-poster with its Tempur-Pedic mattress. The last detail provided by a nightstand card promoting its merits.

THE ACADEMY

Christopher is cuddled and unconscious beside me, his front to my back. His arm lies loose over my side. Nothing could be more perfect.

Just inches from my head, a digital clock informs in angry neon. It's late. Or early.

Depending on your perspective.

Almost five.

I'll be lucky if Winter hasn't called the cops. Despite this, it's hard to summon the energy to care. Let alone expend the calories needed to abandon bed and boy.

He shifts. Losing his warmth is an icy reminder of all I have to do. Reality is black coffee, gulped before it even cools. My heart starts thumping like I'm back in the basement. I'm surprised it doesn't wake him up.

I slip from the sheets. I feel better than any human has a right to. There's no headache, no fizzy tummy. I drank the equivalent of a six-pack last night and I feel just fine. There's no pride there, more like dismay.

Beneath my bare feet the carpeting feels new and clean. I'm pretty sure neither of us looked at the thermostat last night. We had other things on our minds, better ways of staying warm.

Quietly shutting the door behind me, I flick on the light in the outer room. My clothes litter the sofa and the floor; my knapsack occupies the coffee table. I'm not ready to get dressed. Instead, I crank the heat to 80. I slip the blueprint from my purse and put it in inside Jacob's file—still untouched since my basement interment.

Guilt finally catches up with me. I used last night to forget. I drank and I screwed and Sheila is still missing.

JACOB'S BODY

"Going for a run?"

I manufacture a smile even as my pulse hits triple digits. "*Of course*. I'm totally dressed for it."

"I see that." His leer is so out of character that I have to laugh.

His hair is bed-headed, his eyes sleepy. He'd look like a little boy if it weren't for his body. I'm as focused on him as he is on me. When I hugged him in the music room, his layers concealed his transformation. But last night, I could feel how much muscle he's gained. Right now, he's only wearing the boxers I gave him last Valentine's Day, the ones with tiny red hearts.

I ache.

But why has he been lifting weights? When I left, he was still a skinny prodigy, but now he's like some action hero prepping for next summer's blockbuster.

I think about Sheila. Her most recent cover was sexier, revealing more skin in softer lighting. Is it the same for boys? Do they need to look hot to sell classical music to the masses? I feel oddly jealous about my boyfriend debuting his six-pack along with his album.

I want to ask him about all this, but I can't. If I start asking him questions, he might return the favor.

I've never been shy about my body around Christopher. Yet as I move toward him, I'm less conscious of being naked than I am of the purple islands populating my skin, the circle from the doorknob branded on my left hip. I feel awkward and uncomfortable as he pulls me closer.

When we kiss, I imagine a different world. I think about inhabiting a place where there is a normal love life, the only stress my Conservatory audition.

THE ACADEMY

How amazing that would be.

He stops kissing me. "Casey, is something up?"

Instead of answering, I push him back toward the messy bed. It's the best way I know to make sure he forgets the question.

CHAPTER ELEVEN

I dress quickly. Christopher and I leave, a sleepy desk clerk's curious gaze following us out the door. Along the eastern sky, false dawn colors the horizon. We're quiet.

Inside the Rover, Christopher doesn't bother with music. The only cars on the road are headed in the opposite direction, toward distant ski slopes.

Despite the heater, I'm shivering. When we reach the school's southern entrance, Christopher pulls over right inside the gate.

Security lights reveal his unhappiness. "What's going on?"

"Oh not much. Other than I have an audition I'm not ready for and Sheila was helping me but chose last week to leave for China. All of which I would have shared if you weren't such a sexy distraction."

He shakes his head. "*Seriously.* Your audition doesn't explain why you were wasted last night."

"I was at a dinner with my boyfriend. It's a freaking holiday and I worked all week..."

"Or why I showed up to a girlfriend who looked like she spent the day on a road crew."

"A what?"

"Did you skip school to dig ditches?"

"No, I..."

He puts his hand on my arm and says, "I want you to succeed. That's all I want, all any of us wants."

I shove his hand away. "Who is 'us'? My mom? Keifer? The headmaster? I need you to be my boyfriend, not my dad!"

I bite back the tears, the anger. Because I need *my dad* to be my dad. Unfortunately, that's a permanent vacancy.

He takes my hand. I try pulling away but he holds tighter. His hand is freezing. I start to remember the crazy dream that woke me up, kissing Jacob's death-chilled lips.

I squeeze my eyes closed, warding off the image as I rest my head on Christopher's shoulder.

"If you don't want to go to the Conservatory, don't go," he says, stroking my hair. "I'm not going to love you any less. Believe me, I know what it's like to want something different from what you've been programmed for. But don't quit because you're scared."

"That's not it."

"Then what is it?"

I'm not confessing, not now, not to him. What can he possibly do other than have me committed?

"I'm *fine*. Okay? I used the holiday to do research for a class project. *In the woods.* If you want me to act like a girl and spend two hours getting ready before you show, then at least let me know we have a date."

"Good point."

"Now, baby, please take me back to my dorm before Winter organizes a search party."

He smiles, and when I kiss him, I know my fable has worked.

In the lobby, the alarm has already been disabled for the early risers. Despite the creeping dawn, hallway shadows speed me toward my room. Slipping off my shoes at the stairs, I pad up the flights to the third floor. My door is unlocked. Despite everything, I'm happy to be home, to enter my room confident my absence has gone unnoticed.

    I'm digging for clean clothes when there's a knock on my door. Winter does not look happy.

CHAPTER TWELVE

"Is it a boy?" Winter smooths her smart skirt as she sits on Sheila's former bed. Her eyes reveal more than just concern. I detect something like longing.

I nod. I look well used and dressed for the walk of shame. There's no sense lying.

My housemother offers a thin smile. "It's almost always a boy."

"He… Christopher got me through a lot. Sheila leaving wasn't like when my dad died, but it hasn't been easy either."

"I know. I felt like she helped you with more than music; I could see you getting more confident. Not to mention it sucks when a friend leaves without so much as a text."

"Not that I'd get one here."

"Exactly," she says with a laugh. "I know you think I don't understand, but I do. I was in college when I was your age. You're practically an adult. But you still have to follow the same rules as everyone else."

"Like Sheila did?"

She shakes her head but I know my shot has landed. Winter stretches her arms, adjusts her silk blouse. I've never seen her this shiny. "I saw you play once."

"Really?" For some weird reason this makes me happy. Not as happy as I was at The Waverly, but it's definitely the best I've felt since my feet touched Academy property.

"Really." She stands, watches as I put my jacket on a hanger. "It was a July Fourth—some Boston Pops thing. What were you, fourteen?"

"*Thirteen*. I was with my dad." I say this as I shut the closet door and sit on my bed.

Remembering him is always a sadness, but this memory is so bright it overwhelms darker emotions. It was a last-minute deal. Mom tried to talk him out of it. We'd made plans. *Family plans.* Instead she spent her holiday backstage in a tent while I got to play cello ten feet from Yo-Yo Ma. Afterward, I was with my parents and the performers, watching fireworks explode over the Charles.

Winter has been watching me this whole time, watching me think about my father. "It was a long time ago."

"Not for me. For me, it could be yesterday."

"What do you mean?"

"Yo-Yo Ma was amazing, Casey. Your dad was amazing. But you? *You* were the one I remember."

"That's crazy."

"No. *It isn't.* See, I'd been here for a while and I was starting to think about trying for an orchestra again. Watching you play made me realize I was never going to make it as a pianist."

"Oh my God, that's horrible. I'm *so* sorry."

"Don't be. I'm not. You saved me years of playing at third-rate malls and cheesy bars while wondering why I couldn't land a decent audition. And it wasn't just your technique—although you had that in spades. It was... passion. *Passion* and precision, a pretty unbeatable combo."

"Christ, Winter, you're talking about me like I'm Sheila."

"What the hell does that mean?"

"My dad was incredible. Thanks to him, I got to play some pretty cool venues and meet some pretty awesome people. But I'm no prodigy. My mother is the reason I never recorded an album but I'm pretty sure no one would have bought it if I had."

"That's a load of bull. Sheila was...Sheila is awesome." I look hard at her when she corrects her tense but she ignores this. Instead she sits back down on the abandoned bed and smiles at me.

I realize I've been unconsciously twisting the edge of my sheet this whole time. I smooth it down as she continues. "Sheila is on a different road. That's all. I'm sure you feel like people treat you differently because your father was Julius Barnes. Maybe they do, maybe you get to go to the front of the line sometimes. But you're proving yourself now. Tanking your first shot at the Conservatory could be a blessing."

"Right." Nice blessing. Besides being shipped to Siberia, I'm pretty sure someone at my new school is stealing teenagers.

"I'm serious, Casey. You need to find a way to believe in yourself. Because Sheila never had to go through anything like you did after your father died. That means something. Assuming you actually work through it all and make it to the other side."

"And what's waiting for me there? On the other side, I mean?" I say it like a joke but Winter doesn't smile.

"I'm not writing you up. This is your freebie—getting nailed for a curfew violation isn't going to help you at the C on Friday."

"Thank you." I stand as she does, taking a deep breath when she heads to the door. She's left it open. My floor is silent.

"Winter, were you here when Amber Perkins was killed?"

She turns back, her face pale, her expression set. She nods. "I started right before the summer program, at what is now Boys' B. Amber was in my dorm."

"What was she like?"

"I've known a lot of talented musicians, but she was one of the best." She smiles. "Amber could have given you and Sheila a run for your money. But her demons caught up with her."

"What do you mean?"

"I was new. I let things slide. Amber was troubled."

"Like me?" I say with a smile I don't really feel.

"No, *not* like you," she replies in a harsh whisper. "The Academy seems to be working for you. It never worked for Amber."

"Worked for her?"

"It's supposed to be like this, it's designed to promote focus. Leaving home, leaving cities, leaving… everything. You're left with nothing but your talent." I'm about to say something when she looks hard at me. "You know, Sheila was asking me the same types of questions right before you moved in."

"I know. Darlene told me." It's a pale lie but I'd rather not admit how deep this has gotten.

As if she's read my mind, Winter warns, "You can't afford to divide your discipline, Casey. Sheila could get away with slacking off, you can't. *Not* because you're any less talented, but because Sheila has already been admitted to her first-choice school."

"I know."

"I'll say this. I've never experienced small-town, small-minded prejudice before. After Amber went missing, after her body… Every local thought someone from here was responsible. Which is crazy."

"Why?"

"*Why?* Because the stuff you're dealing with, Amber went through all that and more when she was *ten*. It seemed like whenever I visited Elba's Books or Al's, Amber would be strolling the sidewalk with a different guy. They all looked town. Most were older. She started missing curfews; she looked like she'd been drinking. I should have talked to Mr. Collins or at least written her up."

"Why didn't you?"

"Because I was naive. I really thought if I gave her time, I'd have a chance to get through to her. But that never happened."

She starts to head toward her room, but then freezes in the hallway. "I hope you understand what a big deal it is that I'm letting you get away with this."

"I do. I promise I'm not going to screw up again."

I shut the door, wondering if her letting Sheila slide cost my dorm mate's life like it did Amber's.

I lock the door, then double-check it. I *don't* do it three times, I'm *not* OCD. But Winter's trip down memory lane reminds me that in twenty-four hours I've broken into school property, stolen school property, pilfered vodka, and violated curfew.

Maybe my focus isn't perfect, but I really do want to get into the Conservatory. After everything that's happened in Vermont, New York City is going to seem downright serene.

CHAPTER THIRTEEN

I soon realize why the school file on Jacob is so heavy. It's crammed with evaluations and recommendations, part of what would have been an application package to an elite music college if he hadn't disappeared.

I carefully set aside letters of praise from the headmaster and the school's first piano instructor. I skim others contributed by names I recognize, people my father knew. I also quickly work my way through grades and course information—although not so quickly that I don't see how Jacob was taking way more advanced classes and doing better at them than me.

It's weird—the waterworks were shut down when my father was buried. Now, thinking about the potentially brilliant futures ripped from Jacob and Amber, my eyes well up.

Would Jacob have gotten trashed before a major audition? Despite being "troubled," would Amber?

I reach a stack of pictures. Not of students, these are black-and-white copies of photos. There's a shot of the barn that became the dining hall. There are pages devoted to the old house that became my dorm. The last bunch are focused on clearings and other vacant areas, including a strip of land that looks like the final resting place for old farm equipment.

At the bottom of the pile is a map.

It has been folded and re-folded so many times that when I spread it across the floor it tears a bit along a crease. A grid covers lines that look like roads and dark shaded areas that might be mountains. Between these are perfect squares that might be buildings, and less perfect rectangles drawn in red marker that might be plans. Beside the red squares, numbers six places past the decimal have been jotted down.

In the far corner, hard against one of the mountains, is yet another red rectangle. I stop breathing for a moment. Scrawled beside it are the words: *Auto Graveyard... Jacob?*

They're in Sheila's handwriting.

CHAPTER FOURTEEN

Everything is different in the morning.

For weeks, I've barely been awake in time to make my first class, let alone breakfast. Too wired, too scared to sleep, I take a shower. Which I actually have to wait for. I'm grateful for the crowd, the memory of Jacob's "visit" still fresh. Paranoid, I don't leave anything important in my room. I don't let my knapsack out of my sight, hanging it from a hook in the stall. Then I check to make sure the door is locked before sliding back the curtain and stepping beneath the spray.

As the water hits my skin, I let my thoughts drift.

Had Sheila figured out where Jacob was buried? I'm not sure how she made the connection between the teen's disappearance and an unused tract of land. The words *Auto Graveyard* are equally confusing. It didn't say *Jacob's grave.* It's a reference to… what? A place where cars are buried? Did she go there before she wrote the entry or figure it out online?

Was Jacob killed there? My hallucination showed Collins with a gun but I never heard a shot or saw him pull the trigger. And why was the file still in the cabin? Did Sheila return it? Or did Collins find it in the jumble of her things that I dug through last night? If the headmaster found it, why wouldn't he just burn the thing?

I've been blessed with good timing lately. I only learned about Amber after discovering the picture in Sheila's journal. Not long after I took it from her violin case, I bumped into Collins. The next day, Sheila's case was gone. Later, he'd asked if I had anything of hers—the point so clear he may as well have been asking to read it.

Maybe my timing at the cabin was equally blessed. Collins (who else could it have been?) could have been planning to destroy Jacob's file. After it wasn't found among Sheila's things, they would have guessed she'd returned it. Which means the person who locked me in the basement had shown up planning to take it. Instead, he'd heard me digging around and made a quick decision. With me out of the picture, he'd have the time to do what he needed to do.

Drying off, I wonder what happened while I was trapped. Did Sheila's kidnapper kill her or just move her? Is the map a crucial clue? Will it help me find Jacob's body?

Or will it lead me to Sheila's?

I don't want to think about the last part.

Instead, I dress quickly in my room while forming a plan. The blueprint suggests something—maybe Jacob's body, maybe another clue—is in the basement. I'm convinced the vision in the shower means that he was killed here. Unfortunately, there's no way to test that theory with everyone milling around. So, if my auto graveyard search is a bust, I guess I'll be excavating well past dark. *Lovely.*

I'm grateful for the map but there's no way I can read it. I need to find something suitable for a girl who's lived her whole life with GPS. Ideally something with pictures and large arrows. I'd go back to Elba's, but considering Collins' recent prohibition, I don't want to leave campus so soon after Winter's leniency.

Downstairs, I think about knocking on Darlene's door. Besides still being hella early, I realize I don't want to just show her the map and the blueprint. After all, she's the reason I found the file in the first place. Besides not getting her into trouble, I actually want to impress her. To do that, I need to learn more. Then I will tell her everything.

Unfortunately, the library doesn't open until ten on weekends. With nothing better to do, I head to the dining hall and manage a decent breakfast. Afterward, I realize one reason I don't like big meals. I'm groggy. If it weren't for Sheila, I'd take a nap and not wake up until two. Instead, I stroll toward the library, planning on joining the handful of motivated students who hang around the entrance right before it opens.

The headmaster changes my plans.

I have to pass the music building on the way to the library. He's walking toward the entrance, his face unreadable. My stomach churns as I contemplate diving behind some bushes. I wonder if Winter kept her promise or if Collins knows about my night off campus with my boyfriend.

I'm frozen, unable to make a decision. Which is when he turns, smiles, and calls to me from the front steps. "Casey, look at you, all bright-eyed and bushy tailed."

"Yes, sir," I reply, the "sir" rolling around in my mouth like a dirty penny. His happy demeanor recently is unfamiliar. He smiles at other students, at parents, at donors. With me, he usually alternates between disappointment, pity, and barely concealed flashes of anger. Trying to stay on his good side, I add, "Christopher wanted me to tell you how much he enjoyed talking about music with you. Most people are pushing him to stay classical and you're one of the few who appreciates electronic."

"I've never been very interested in the divisions between low-brow and high-brow. Did you know in the 1950s, middle-class families watched opera on TV? It's why the world has *Amahl and the Night Visitors*."

I have no idea why he's giving me a history lesson but I'm suddenly more irritated than scared. Maybe I *am* hung over.

He's still droning on. "… tell Christopher how pleased I was to meet him. Just wish we could have recruited him."

"Ha. I'm sure."

"It is nice to see you getting in some practice before noon."

I hate that he knows my schedule. Instead of heading to the library and maybe finding Sheila, I'm forced to trail him up the stairs of the music building.

At any other school a student bound for the library on a Saturday morning would earn compliments. *Not here.* I can say I have a project due, but knowing Collins he'll disprove that fib by lunch. Besides, any excuse guarantees a lecture on "time management." Since I can't do anything else, I resign myself to heading toward my practice room.

It would be simple to sneak out in five minutes. But seeing the headmaster feels like an omen. How many times have I promised not to let anything interfere with my audition? My lies are bubbling and boiling over. A bit of honesty will cool them down.

Besides, most of the scary things in here have happened at night. After getting the day's prep out of the way in the bright light of morning, I'll start my afternoon with some internet sleuthing.

I work through angst with Schubert and a bit of Bach before finding a happy place with Joplin. An hour later, I take a moment. The second I do, there's a sharp rap on the pane in the center of the door. I almost launch my cello into the carpet. Keifer's face is framed within the glass. After setting my instrument inside its case, I open the door.

My teacher is dressed in a faded denim shirt and torn jeans, like he's been gardening. His hair is poofed up so high he resembles Einstein in that old poster. His eyes look tired.

"Sorry to disturb your work, Casey," he apologizes with a scratchy voice.

"Just finishing up."

"*Excellent.* I was wondering if you'd like to go over your audition piece. I had a faculty meeting cancel at the last moment, so I have some free time."

I do not. The library is open, and motivated academics are queuing up. And I don't want to be searching for Sheila in the dark.

"That would be awesome."

CHAPTER FIFTEEN

I should be distracted. Jacob's ghost looms large in my brain, but I push that aside. Instead, my fingers guide the bow while my mind focuses on a single opportunity. Everything that isn't ragtime, that isn't a hundred-year-old composition of humor and enthusiasm, disappears.

I play "Easy Winners" over and over. I start anew before the last notes have time to fade. Mr. Keifer remains silent until our hour is almost up. Then reality intrudes.

His eyes brighten as he holds up a hand to keep me from playing the same tune for the 38th time. "That was truly inspired, Casey. Every note was better than the last."

"Thank you," I say quietly. Guilt about Sheila returns. Once again, I've forgotten about her. Forgotten about Jacob. Anxiety crescendos.

"When we do this again on Monday, I'm going to stop you. *Repeatedly.* You probably won't be interrupted during your audition, but I want you to get comfortable with the unexpected."

I return my cello and bow to the case, thinking about how the unexpected isn't what did me in the last time. I mean, it's not exactly surprising that if you drink a small pond of alcohol you'll be hung over and spinning the next day.

"Still, I'm glad I let you play the piece a few times. It's a good way to get a feel for how well you know the material."

"And?"

"When we first met in August, you told me you were abandoning your first audition piece for something you'd never played before. I was understandably concerned. It made sense that you'd want to show the selection committee something new but the Joplin seemed drastic. Plus, well, Sheila can be a very persuasive young woman."

"I know."

"It's a complex piece to master in so short a time."

This echoes my every insecurity.

Keifer stops and rubs a hand over his beard. He stares at me. I try not to stare at my shoes. "My worries were unfounded." He smiles. "I don't say this very often, but I was wrong."

"Really?" I feel my own smile develop.

"*Really.* I'm a bit chagrined, to be honest," he says, opening the door. "If the Conservatory says no again, I'm going to stop sending any more of my students their way, because they've clearly lost their collective minds."

I laugh at this but the giggle pulls up something else. Leaning forward, I give him an awkward hug. His faded shirt smells spicy and clean. It's a scent from every time my father held me.

Then I'm bawling. Full-out, head against Keifer's shoulder. It's a good minute before I can hiccup myself back into control. He's obviously uncomfortable, his arms stiff at his sides.

I wipe my eyes angrily with the sleeve of my shirt and glance toward the door. A girl waits at the threshold. My vision is blurry but I make out bare legs and too-short shorts. I wonder if Amber has enjoyed my little meltdown.

I grab my knapsack and cello case, mumbling "Thank you" over my shoulder. When I reach the hallway, I look around. My observer is gone.

CHAPTER SIXTEEN

At the Music Building's exit doors, I pause with my fingers on the handle. I'd played Schubert's "Ave Maria" at my father's memorial and again at my floundering conservatory audition. The night after Sheila disappeared, I heard its first faint notes inside my practice room—despite the soundproofing. I trailed cello music down three flights of stairs to the first-floor rehearsal hall. The music had grown deafening but when I arrived at its source there was nothing but a trio of Arts on the bare stage.

That was the first time I heard Amber Perkins playing. I'm certain it was her. I know it just like I know today is at least the second time I've seen her. She was murdered ten years ago in early summer. Her clothing betrays the seasons.

I have to get to the auto graveyard. There has to be something there about either Amber or Jacob.

But first I want to search the rehearsal hall. The doors are propped open, the seats vacant. I don't see anyone, real or otherwise.

Onstage, an empty chair waits before a single music stand. Across its seat lies a bow identical to my own.

I let out a tiny yelp, and Collins's voice drifts up from the orchestra pit. He says my name so clearly I assume he's seen me. I almost answer when I hear Winter's voice.

"She's fine." I bite my lip to keep from gasping.

"I ran into her outside earlier. I thought inviting her last night would be motivational but she looked distracted. Off… Something."

My stomach clenches as I wonder if he's guessed I'd been drinking. I hold my breath as he asks, "Are you sure Darlene has been keeping an eye on her?"

"*Positive.* She's been with her pretty much every minute she isn't in class or practicing. I think you're going to be very pleased."

"I hope so. Casey is going to have a hard time overcoming that debacle of an audition."

"She'd just lost her father."

"Anyone who cares about music lost someone when Julius died."

I'm so angry, I almost want them to know I'm here. From this angle I can't see them, but I imagine they are ducked down in the first row. I'm not sure why they are hanging out in this vacant auditorium, why they chose this venue to discuss my merits.

"…ten years is long enough to be a housemother."

"True. It's crazy you still call it that."

"You'd prefer *resident advisor*? *Housemother* is a tad old fashioned, I'll admit, but it best describes your role. You truly are 'in loco parentis.' You provide our young women with guidance, discipline…"

"A strategy to avoid going from being youngest in your class at Juilliard to playing Chopin Tuesday afternoons at the Springlake Mall."

I hear Collins laugh. It's an ugly sound. When he speaks again, his voice is lower, throaty. "Well, Darlene's video really helped. I knew it would."

"*Wait.* What are you talking about? I just auditioned."

"And I told you that was a formality. They watched the footage of you performing that song you wrote and well… That's why I had you meet me here. I just got off the phone with my friend. He told me you can plan on joining their Master's program next fall. He even thinks he can get you an RA position."

"Oh my God, Tim, thank you."

And then I hear something that can only be one thing. It's one of those unmistakable sounds, like a bone breaking. I wish it could be something else, but it isn't. They are kissing.

My head is a kaleidoscope, a swirling pinwheel of red and orange. I race outside, overwhelmed by disgust, anger… and betrayal.

I knew Darlene was telling Winter things about me, but I still wanted to trust her. After she told me about the cabin and the school's files, I really believed there were things she wouldn't share. I never guessed that she was faking friendship, trailing me and reporting to the housemother like an informant in some cop show.

At this point, Winter seems more loyal. At least she's kept my time with Christopher a confidence.

CHAPTER SEVENTEEN

I wait almost an hour before a computer frees up. Most schools wired their dorms last century. Here, parents pay extra so their offspring can study in medieval conditions.

I haven't been online in days. It's after one and I have research to do, but I still feel bad not messaging my friends, my mom.

Getting what I need is easier than I expected. After plugging the coordinates beside Sheila's note into a search engine, I find images for dozens of options, including maps I can actually read. But I've gone hours without caffeine and my little sob fest has left me exhausted. If I try to scribble this stuff down, I'm bound to screw up.

Since the four computers on my table share a single printer, I stand as soon as I've given the command. I wait impatiently for my pages. Of course no one pays attention. The others are so focused on their rare web fix, they wouldn't notice giant turtles mating in the biography section.

I slip the printouts into my knapsack. It's now a repository for all things macabre: the book on local ghosts that Sheila ordered, paid for and never picked up at Elba's; her journal; the newspaper article from June on the tenth anniversary of Amber's murder. *Jacob's file and the blueprint.* And now a map to the auto graveyard.

Returning to my monitor, I examine photographs and satellite views. I find a shot of the area Sheila circled.

The photo is of a clearing, with green leaves and brown grass. It looks like it was taken on the hottest day of the summer. Abandoned tractors appear to be wilting. Antique forklifts display melting seats and bleeding rust.

Trading sleep for Christopher and cello catches up with me. I nod off with my face in my right hand.

My subconscious spins a black night absent moon or stars. It also manufactures the shell of an old Mustang. The muscle car's sharp edges recall vehicles I'd seen whenever we drove through rougher parts of Boston.

I approach it eagerly, unconcerned as I settle into the passenger seat. Despite the elements and age, the leather is comfortable.

Jacob gets in beside me. He pretends to drive, a boy discovering a new plaything. I smile as he apes a getaway, steering hard to the left and the right. I follow these movements, pretending along with him.

My ghost boy is handsome and lively. Nothing about his appearance suggests he's been worm food for twenty years. But when he puts his hand on my own, his skin is ice cold.

Despite this, I'm not afraid. He trusts me. He knows I'm trying.

Jacob takes his other hand from the steering wheel. He points through the space where the windshield would be, his finger aimed down and to the left. I understand.

Leaving the car is more frightening than sitting beside its undead occupant. I step carefully, fingers tracking the hood in case I stumble. Jacob hasn't moved. He's still indicating a space just in front of the driver's side.

The pile of dirt is higher than the front bumper. I lean toward it. There's an impression in the ground. About a foot down lies a square of plywood. It begins to move. I step back.

JACOB'S BODY

The plank is dislodged, flying up a few feet before landing beside another car. When I lean back in, I can see the hole. I can't see the bottom.

A thin voice drifts up. *"Help!"*

It's Sheila!

I step closer.

And then I am falling...

I startle awake. No one is looking at me, which means I managed to avoid screaming or snoring. I wipe drool from my chin with the back of my hand. It's time to go.

CHAPTER EIGHTEEN

It's after three and lengthening shadows creep from the trees. Finding a secluded bench, I dig for the printouts in my knapsack. One shows the school's buildings. The path I want connects to the nature trail, the head of which lies between the music building and dining hall. The nature trail is featured on The Academy's website, but the overgrown path is noted only on crudely drawn maps and archival blog posts.

I've been on the school's nature trail just a few times. Despite keeping an eye out, I almost pass it. The entrance is shabby, the sign concealed by shrubbery. I push past a scramble of brush, emerging on a flat dirt lane the width of a city sidewalk. It's darker here and I soon see why. Most of the trees around campus are maple or birch. Their barren branches don't block sunlight. The trail cuts through a dense forest of evergreens.

If Sheila hadn't taken me under her wing, I'd be more familiar with this trail. If I'd been totally on my own, I would have spent a fair amount of time strolling and contemplating.

Ahead of me, scattered couples climb a gentle hill—the feet of some of the steepest mountains in New England. Nearby, three male Arts collect moss and leaves like mother birds in springtime. Do the Arts always travel in trios?

There's a reason the path isn't on the school's website. It's a conduit to an almost forgotten place, an obscure destination for couples who have vastly different ideas about communing with nature than the ones hiking away the afternoon. One blog promised the path was before the hill, so I pace out 100 strides before turning around, walking almost all the way back to the nature trail's entrance, then repeating my effort. I do this several times, getting closer and closer to the hill, but feeling farther and farther from my destination.

I'm screwed, I think, but keep trying.

Focusing on the ground, I look for the smallest sign: a place where a gap was designed, some unnatural space in the brush.

Finally, I find what I'm looking for. Pushing a clutch of briars aside with the bottom of my jacket, I lean forward. A thin, mucky line cuts between the pines. My heart speeds up. This is it. I'm sure of it.

I press through, turning my body and—as my jacket lifts up, exposing bare skin—getting rewarded with a scratch across my stomach. The path veers to the left and then… Nothing. A rotting tree blocks my way, and on the other side there's nothing but thorny brush—all aligned as if planted to make this passage impossible.

As I back onto the path, a returning couple confirms this.

"That doesn't go anywhere," a blond girl who faintly reminds me of Sheila offers. Deflated, I return her smile. "Thanks, I figured. Is there another one nearby? Maybe a connection?"

The guy she's with, just as blond, just as cute, shakes his head. "No, it's all overgrown. Definitely not a place you want to get lost in."

They shrug past me, destined toward campus and the sort of Saturday plans I enjoyed before missing girls, ghosts, and homicidal headmasters became the stars in my headspace.

THE ACADEMY

Someone has to know more. The school either planted or allowed sticker bushes to take over, helping keep students from trekking through the woods, but they wouldn't be a deterrent for everyone. Most would view a clearing stuffed with broken machinery as an eyesore, but to some isolated teenagers, it would be as inviting as a wardrobe leading to Narnia.

CHAPTER NINETEEN

I feel defeated. Walking by the Headmaster's Residence, I note how quiet it seems, how empty after last night's festivities. Just then, Collins materializes. He's standing outside my dorm, leaning on the bench by the sidewalk. A pair of girls stop and start chatting breezily, picking his brain no doubt for New York stories or audition tips. He's focused on them, which means I'm still safe. I wait to cross the road, not wanting to go past him.

I'm not sure why he would be waiting for me, what has changed since he saw me a few hours ago. It makes more sense he'd be waiting for Winter. Except that seems blatant even for him.

"Meditating?"

I jump at Emily's voice. She's sporting shiny leggings and a halter, an outfit as ready for the weather as North Face gear on Miami Beach. The shorter the days get, the redder her hair seems. She removes a pair of enormous blue-tinted sunglasses; her light brown eyes faintly sparkling with mischief. Emily has the untroubled face of a girl who only worries about music and clothes, in that order. The more you get to know her, the more beautiful she becomes. It's as if looks and personality could merge into something completely different and indefinable.

"Uhmm…no. Debating."

Usually Emily races by, her New York stroll on full display. This afternoon, she lingers. She seems calmer. Maybe just in comparison to me.

"You don't look like a girl who spent time with a boy as pretty as Christopher."

"Maybe because I got home at five a.m."

Emily whistles. "What a naughty girl! And after Darlene convinced me to ease up on you about blowing off practice."

"It's fine. Winter let me off with a warning and Mr. Keifer just told me I'm ready for Friday's audition."

"*Seriously*? Wow, Sheila said once he wouldn't compliment a student to talk them off the ledge of a building."

"I know. If I wasn't so sleep deprived I'd be doing the happy dance."

"Come on! I'm solo tonight and campus is giving me the downs. Let's celebrate."

Instead of protesting, I let Emily take my elbow and steer me away from our dorms.

The drive is different somehow. I've come into town more times this week than I usually do in a month. I think about how Emily never saw the ghost in the crosswalk the other day, how she drove right through her. Can anyone else see them? Other than Sheila?

Emily drives an ancient Mercedes that hasn't seen a wash since August. The inside, however, is pristine, with seats and an instrument panel that look transplanted from a more recent model. The Bose system blasts a Selena Gomez song that was "my most favorite ever" when I was nine. Emily picks up the tune, matching pitch almost perfectly. I sing quietly, happily transported until we pass the converted feed store, now home to *The Daily Herald*. She notices that I've stopped singing and turns down the volume.

"Was it fun time traveling?" Emily asks. "Being inside a newspaper, I mean."

I laugh a little. "That would be uncomfortable, actually. But yeah, the *newsroom* was interesting." Emily must get enough of a signal in town to check her sites. Those of us without cars make do at the library. It's why we pore over the papers delivered to our dorms. When you're cut off from the world, you'll do anything to reconnect.

Turning, I look back at the offices, now dark. "You'll never guess what they call the place where they keep back issues."

"What?"

"The morgue."

"Wow. Scary."

"It was." I look away from the building now, feeling lightheaded. I think about Jacob's brief appearance while I waited for the back issue with the article about Amber's disappearance. I'm startled when I realize Emily is parking, guiding her car into a space half a block from our destination. Unbuckling my seatbelt, I add, "The woman in charge had blue hair and stays underground the whole day. She remembered Sheila."

"Of course she did. Your roomie is very memorable." Emily exits, her brisk city pace returning as she rushes down the walk. I trail, bothered by how deserted the street is.

Inside, old black-and-white photos of happy couples sharing ice cream and playing the jukebox conjure happier times. Some were taken in the 1950s, when Al's was a glistening converted railroad dining car and the top spot in town. It's no longer shiny, but it's just as popular. On Saturday nights it gets so crowded, a line forms. Emily and I snag a booth just in time.

The conversation doesn't grow serious until we've finished our milkshakes. I'm not used to "celebrating" with frozen dairy products. Considering the temperature and how much skin she's showing, they seem like a bad idea. But Emily doesn't even shiver.

"Sheila really believed in you. I hope you get in."

"Thanks. Me too. I know you thought I was slacking, that I'm expecting Manhattan C to take me over some talented kid because of my last name."

Emily actually blushes and shakes her head. "I was a B last time we were here. *Sorry*. I get a little insane right before a performance and my Berklee audition is a hundred times more important."

"I get it. Believe me."

"I head down on Monday, so tomorrow I'll be a nutty stress ball again. But I wanted to give my head a break and when I saw you…"

"You figured you could pump me for dirty details?"

"Ha. I figured I could save you from our lurking Head."

"You've noticed too?"

"Are you kidding? Like, why's he watching your dorm? Isn't that Winter's job?"

"Thanks for looking out… Seriously, I hardly ever saw Collins before last week and now he's… I don't know. *Ubiquitous*." Emily doesn't say anything so I add, "It means…"

"I know what it means. Jeesh, I'm taking the same tests you are. You have to realize, if you get in it makes the school look good. Which makes him look good. Plus, he did catch you skipping practice to investigate Amber Perkins."

I squeeze a napkin and try to take a cleansing breath. She's not wrong, but her defense of Collins is unnerving.

"So, how's that going, by the way?" I look up from my napkin ball. She seems genuinely interested as she asks, "Your murder investigation? Darlene said something about a cabin?"

Of course she did. If Darlene had more online time, there'd probably be a whole Insta story. Thinking about how I can't trust her makes me sad in a way that's different—sharper—than all the other sadnesses weighing me down.

"Well…" I remember yesterday, how I was thinking that I can't do this alone. I have to trust someone. Maybe Emily can help. "I did find something." It takes a moment of digging before I can extricate the map from my tightly stuffed knapsack. I set it down on the table. "I think Sheila figured out where Jacob is buried."

"Jacob?"

"The farmer's kid, the first one to go missing?"

"Right."

I turn the page around so it's facing her and tap the circle. "That's Sheila's handwriting."

"Wow. That's nuts. And you found this in the cabin?"

"In Jacob's file. With a bunch of photos—I think a lot of things to do with his dad were just shoved in there."

"It doesn't prove anything."

"I know. But what if Sheila went there?"

"And was what, murdered? Fell down a well?"

"I don't know. That's just it. I still don't know anything and I spent all afternoon looking for a way to get up there. Instead, the path I found was covered in thorn bushes. Looked like it was purposely planted, you ask me."

"I'm sure it was. Trust me, that 'auto graveyard' is a tetanus shot waiting to happen."

"Wait. You've been up there?"

She nods with an odd little smile. "Sophie and I went there a few times last semester, before I got my car. It's really scary, even in daylight. But we needed"—she winks at me—"privacy."

I look at her. She's not the first gay person I've been friends with, not by a long shot. But stereotypes are weird things. Emily is this shiny fashionista, like the blonde on that old show about the missing girl. Of course, I read somewhere that the actress who played her is dating a woman, so…

I guess I'm quiet for too long because Emily says, "You look shocked."

"No, I mean, it's just…"

"I don't look gay?" She says this in a harsh whisper, the smile gone. My words are jumbling together as I stutter an apology before she laughs. "Chill, I'm just giving you grief. I'm not embarrassed or anything, but Sophie's parents live like an hour away and they're always dropping by. Shocking that religious freaks would send their darling daughter to a school with restricted Internet and crappy cell coverage."

"Shocking."

"So we keep it on the DL to stop some Academy gossip from spilling the beans."

"Like Darlene," I say, my own whisper as harsh as Emily's was a moment ago.

"Darlene? No, why would you say that? She's a good egg, although to be honest she had a serious girl crush on Sheila."

"Who didn't?" I say.

CHAPTER TWENTY

Bellies full, we head back to the Academy. At the southern gate, Emily waves off my questions as she drives right past. Through gaps in the trees, I follow the lights of campus. Somewhere up there is my dorm. Somewhere up there are the spirits of two teenagers. I can only pray Sheila hasn't joined them. Impatience grows again as I realize our outing is being extended.

Just past The Academy's northern gate, Emily cuts across the road. She turns sharply 180 degrees, so we're facing the school. She shuts off the lights but leaves the engine running. "C'mon," she says.

With her phone set to flashlight, we walk between the culvert and the road. I try not to trip as my mind spins demons in the dark.

"Gotcha!" She leans over and lifts a branch. A faded pink bandanna is tied to it. "We had this whole system. Like with our dorm rooms, when one person wants to have someone over? Anyway, she'd tie this here if she wanted to see me. I'd jog by after classes, before practice. It was fun at first but then I got the car so…"

"Thanks for this." I hadn't thought about looking for a second path to the junkyard.

"No problem. See? Just pull the brush back a bit and…" She raises her light so I can see the narrow footpath ambling toward black. "Do *not* come here at night, it's not worth it, no matter what you think you'll find. Wait until tomorrow."

"Are you worried I'll get attacked by demons?"

"No, silly. *Bears.* I've seen at least two since the weather turned."

Walking from the school parking lot, Emily stops short. I almost run into her. Along the far edge, Collins and Keifer argue beside Keifer's car. It's as ancient as Emily's, an impractical convertible that looks pulled from a Bond movie.

The headmaster's hands go up, his face red under the security lights. Keifer just stands there, his arms folded over his chest. They may be whispering but it's an angry whisper.

"Wonder what's that's all about?"

"No idea, but we should get out of here. I'd rather not get spotted," I say, slinking toward the street.

Emily follows. We're by her dorm when she says, "That guy is such a creeper."

"Didn't we just have this conversation?"

"Not *Collins.* Your cello instructor. Keifer is a grade-A perv."

I don't say anything. There's nothing I *can* say, really. He's always been nice to me; he's never, ever come across as someone I should be nervous being alone in a room with. Except Darlene was freaked when we bumped into him last week. She's not as bold as Emily, she wouldn't tell me why he made her nervous. If the two people Sheila trusted more than anyone else at the Academy share the same bad feelings about Keifer, then I should probably add him to my list of suspects.

CHAPTER TWENTY-ONE

On the way to my room, I struggle mentally. Emily seems sincere—she wants me to get into Manhattan C and even showed me a path to the auto graveyard. But I'm not sure I can take her advice and wait to visit it until tomorrow.

There's mail leaning against my door. Reading the return address makes up my mind. I'm going into the woods. *Tonight.* Because I know what's in the package even before I shut the door behind me and dump its contents onto my bed: the leggings and wool socks and long underwear I've been begging my mom to send me since the nights dipped below freezing.

Emily has helped me more than I could have hoped for. But I haven't been able to convince her that Sheila is in trouble. She doesn't share my suspicion of Collins. I know my cello teacher helped Collins open the school. He's the only other person who has been at The Academy since its inception. Maybe he *is* involved. The thing is, it doesn't really matter. All that matters is finding Sheila. If she's still alive, she's probably endured more than I can imagine. The auto graveyard is my best clue right now, and time is running out. I have clear directions, Darlene's unreliable flashlight, and thanks to my mother, I won't freeze to death.

Putting toe to heel, I remove my dirty sneakers without untying them. Kicking them into the closet, I peel off my inadequate socks. Then I just stand there: bare feet on bare floor. Heat from lower floors usually keeps it warm enough but tonight all I feel are drafts. I take a deep breath before yanking my sweater and long-sleeved T-shirt over my head. The neck snags my hair. I pull harder, shedding hair and tears as my ponytail loosens. Finally freed, I toss the clothes onto the socks and remove my bra. My jeans and underwear follow in one fell swoop. Everything gets booted into the closet.

My reflection stares back at me: a too-thin, too-pale girl framed in the mirror like an art exhibit, someone who looks so much younger than I feel. I take a deep breath, summoning strength I'm not sure I have.

I don't move to get dressed. Instead I stand there, naked and shivering, berating myself for the time spent with Christopher and the meal with Emily and the dozens of other distractions that have kept me from finding Sheila.

This isn't helping.

Sighing, I dig through my dresser for a sports bra. Then I start ripping through plastic and cardboard, nauseated by the strong odor of chemicals. I never wear new things without washing them first. I actually sniff a pair of the leggings, but they just smell like fabric. They are, however, way too tight. I've either put on a few LBs or my mom forgot my size. I drag them up my legs, wincing as they snag the places where I need to shave. My stomach feels pushed up and gross.

The long johns smell like ammonia. Where did Mom get this stuff? I should have taken care of it, ordered clothes online from the library. It's just there's this diminishing part that still wants to be her little girl, still wants her to do things for me. It's not because I'm lazy. I need to be reminded that I'm not an orphan. That there's still one parent looking out for me.

Ignoring my discomfort, I pull on the long johns and waddle to the dresser and then dig out my baggiest pair of jeans. It's still a struggle to get them on and I have to suck in my belly to get them buttoned. My legs may look like hot dogs but they feel protected—like I've put on armor. I'm struck by how hard it is to move.

I have two hours before curfew, long enough to maybe save Sheila's life. Although if I come back with my missing roommate, I'm guessing Winter won't write me up.

I've just put on the long john top and a bulky sweatshirt when Darlene's voice travels through my locked door. "Casey? Hey, my hands are full, can you let me in?"

For a beat, I stare at the wall. I want to ignore her. Except if I do, she'll be talking to Winter before I can lace up my boots. Our housemother is probably in her room, her head heavy with headmaster fantasies.

I can't take the chance of anyone stopping me, so I shove the empty packages into the bottom drawer of my dresser. I try to get the unopened packages in as well. The drawer won't close. "Casey? Are you in there?"

"Just a sec." I kick the new stuff under my bed and race to the door. When I open it, I feel like Darlene and I are closely matched. She too seems dressed for the weather, in bright purple sweats three sizes too big and thick socks she's pulled up over her knees. One hand clutches her boots; her other arm is stuffed with pillows and a comforter.

"Did I catch you in the middle of something?" Her leer looks more out of place on her face than on a toddler's.

She gives me a wink and squeezes my arm as she slips past me, depositing her bedding on the bare bed and her large duffel on my floor. "My roomie is pulling an all-nighter for some trig test on Monday. Do you mind if I crash?"

THE ACADEMY

I want to say no. I have to say no. But the best way to keep Darlene from telling Winter everything is to keep her occupied. I'm just not sure how I'm ever going to find Sheila if her best friend keeps getting in my way.

CHAPTER TWENTY-TWO

After sliding a chair between the beds, Darlene fires up her ancient laptop. It actually has a DVD player. She gives me a stack of discs before extracting a collection of gluten-free snacks and flavored waters from a paper sack.

"Did you get all those at the gym?"

"Totes. Hey, do you want to go there tomorrow?"

"Maybe." She tosses me a bag of kale pretzels, some brand I've never heard of—and I used to hang around Harvard. "You don't have any actual junk food, do you?"

She shakes her head.

"Didn't I see you eating a Pop-Tart?"

"That was a cheat day. I can go down to vending if you want."

"I'm fine." I hate being fake but I don't have a choice. Give and take. She's faking it, too.

Darlene has a grisly collection of gory slasher flicks, but watching one of those guarantees I won't be going into the woods tonight. I settle on a comedy, one funny enough that I actually forget about my life for a minute or three. The lights are off, so she doesn't notice the sweat matting my hair to my forehead.

Darlene is one of those lucky people who can construct a nest anywhere, who can transform any random sofa or floor into her own comfy space. Sheila used to sleep in the bed she's now occupying. I remember her up late with a book light and a magazine or her journal. Darlene lies propped up against the pillows, what looks like a hand-made comforter pulled just below her chin and looking like this has always been hers. She probably wouldn't notice my thermies or even care if she does, but I cover myself with my sleeping bag anyway. I don't feel like answering questions. Plus, if anything at all goes my way tonight, I need to be ready.

We're on our second movie and it's after eleven when Winter knocks. She seems super-happy to see Darlene curled up in Sheila's bed. Their conspiracy to keep me out of trouble is sealed with a glance. I can barely look at my house mom. When I do, I see an image of her with Collins.

It's a good thing I didn't eat the funky pretzels.

As Winter leaves, she starts humming Dvořák's Symphony Number Nine. That's when I know I'll be able to sneak out.

CHAPTER TWENTY-THREE
Sunday
November 13th

In early September when I barely knew Sheila, she told me she had something to show me. It was after midnight, so I figured it would be interesting. I trailed her through the quiet dorm to the lobby.

She smiled while contemplating the alarm. "Winter has a trick. Remember it and you'll never have to worry about curfew."

Watching my dorm mate, I was a combo platter of scared and hopeful. Part of me would have been fine getting expelled, going back to the Boston I missed so much.

Of course with my father dead, the Boston I missed didn't really exist anymore.

"Okay," Sheila whispered. "Winter programs in chord progressions: zero for flat, one for minor, two for major, three for sharp."

I leaned toward her as she entered a code. A second later, the alarm disarmed.

"But how will I know which one she uses?"

Sheila smiled and gave me a quick hug. "It's whatever she's humming." Then she fled into the night.

That time, she returned.

I stare at the alarm. It's after one. If I get this wrong, it will only sound in Winter's room. Thank God for small miracles. At least I won't have to endure the humiliation of getting caught and facing a gaggle of Dorm A residents. Taking a deep breath, I punch in the code.

Time stretches like holiday taffy. Then I'm rewarded with the disarmed beep.

The second movie was halfway over when Darlene finally crashed. I was glad I'd stayed dressed. Besides my knapsack, I retrieved a hoodie, my thickest leather jacket, and hiking boots. I slipped them on in the hallway.

I didn't need the movie for cover. Less than five minutes after falling asleep, Darlene was performing a symphony of snores. Even if Winter wasn't behind our impromptu slumber party, I doubt Morgan is pulling an all-night study session. She probably wanted a holiday from a girl who sounds like a grizzly using a chainsaw.

I open the front door and begin my desolate walk.

The moon shifts behind a cloud. Darlene's flashlight is in my hand, but I keep it off and skirt around the streetlights. My knapsack bangs against my shoulder.

Campus is riskier than the woods. Security roams regularly. Insomniacs gaze out windows. Collins keeps weird hours. If anyone sees me, I'm toast.

Instead of heading to the gate, I slip around the back of Dorm A. The trees are not as dense here. Headlights occasionally cut up from the road. There's no path, no sure way of getting there. I need light but I'm too worried about getting busted. Instead, I shuffle forward slowly. My hands are out in front, pushing branches away. Beneath a cloudy sky, the woods are almost black. I'm almost blind.

I reach a place where it's the same distance between road and dorm; turning back isn't an option. I hear footsteps.

Whoever is behind me is cautious. They are as slow as I am.

Yet the crunch of leaves is unmistakable. I pause. I wait. My breath is loud to my own ears, my face already numb.

A car treks up the road. Its high beams catch a pair of eyes staring right back at me. I inch back, stumbling over a root. My butt hits a patch of mud. I don't feel anything but still gasp, my arms flailing wildly. Somehow the flashlight remains tight in my grasp. I flick it on and aim it at my stalker.

A deer looks at me. She's scrawny, her ribs obvious. Unafraid, she flips her tail a few times before turning and strolling away.

I laugh out loud, loving that I was spooked by Bambi.

With my light on, I reach the road quickly. Trekking beside the culvert, I'm grateful for the flashlight's guidance and hopeful it will offer an early warning to any drunk drivers barreling toward me.

I'm worried I'll miss the marker Emily showed me. Then I see the Academy's north gate and its well-lit guard shack in the distance. A minute later, I spy the pink bandanna. Even without a killer on the prowl, entering the Northeast Kingdom's dense forest in the middle of a winter's night is both dangerous and stupid.

I like to think Sheila would do the same for me.

Of course, she'd be sporting a way better outfit.

I hesitate at the trailhead; consider going back to the dorm, returning tomorrow. This will be more dangerous than anything I've done so far. I'm a city girl. I can only guess how reckless following a barely used path will be.

After a minute of indecision, I get a sign.

The moon shifts from behind the clouds. It's nearly full. I don't even need the flashlight as I push onto the soggy, overgrown path. I spin slowly through the thorns, my head down. They rip at my jacket, grab at my knapsack. A few scratch my hands, prick my fingers.

I don't need gloves. I need a machete.

The forest thickens. Pine trees obscure the moon. The artificial beam is inadequate. I can only see a few yards ahead of me. Past that, darkness is almost total. Branches resemble grasping skeletons. I imagine Jacob's father swinging beside me, pointing the way.

Despite my tiny cuts and deeper wounds, I won't stop. After Dad died, I gave up on the cello and Boston and everything that wasn't Christopher or whatever I could pull from a bottle. Right now, Sheila could be depending on me in a way no one ever has before.

I can't let her down.

I'm certain she has taken this exact path. Maybe she knew about Emily and Sophie; maybe she learned about it in some random way. Maybe she enjoyed her own secret rendezvous long before she started looking for Jacob.

Sheila has always been two steps ahead of me. I trailed her when I was rejected by the school that admitted her. I trailed her to The Academy. No matter what happens, tonight I'm catching up. Because it may sound crazy but for some reason, I know she's still alive.

If I quit, that changes.

CHAPTER TWENTY-FOUR

Online photos didn't do justice to the menagerie of machinery. It's as if Jacob's dad decided that instead of growing corn or wheat, he'd raise tractors and sedans. The moon is fully revealed, but I still play the flashlight over the landscape.

I'm afraid to admit what I'm looking for.

And then I see it.

The Mustang juts from the end of an aisle formed by a dented backhoe and a disintegrating truck. The car doesn't have doors or a hood; I can see the outline of the engine. It didn't show up in a single image search, yet there it is—the vehicle of my nightmare.

Exhaustion swallows me. I collapse into the passenger seat, which is nowhere near as comfy as in my dream. Frigid leather bites my skin despite the layers.

I exhale contrails.

Jacob materializes.

In his worn jeans and T-shirt, with his summer-tan skin and gentle smile, he is as real as the car.

I've dreamed about him twice since he appeared in the shower. This is different. When I look away from him, it isn't from fear. I'm as embarrassed by our last encounter as I would have been with a living boy.

Pushing those thoughts aside, I summon the courage to turn toward him. He's staring. His eyes are deep blue, like the sky after a spring storm. He raises his arm into the space where the windshield would be. I nod as he points, letting him know I understand.

I peer over the hood but don't see a hole. Worse, unlike in my dream, there's no way to move around the front of the car. The bumper presses against the track of the backhoe.

His hand drifts down, settling on my knee. It's colder than the leather seat. Then the air seems to change.

New warmth travels up my leg, burrowing into a tiny space below my belly. I sigh while his hand traces higher.

A tingle emerges from his fingertips before sparking across my entire body. My vision is clouded by misty exhales. As he shifts toward me, I aim the flashlight away. I'm afraid I'll pierce him with its beam. Or worse, that the only thing that feels real right now will disappear.

Instead, I lean toward him, pressing my chest against his. He has substance. I can feel his muscles, the soft hair on his arms. But I don't sense his heartbeat or feel his breath. He smells like vanilla ice cream but I am no longer cold. The uncomfortable position doesn't matter; neither do the pinching long johns twisting up my thighs. And then I'm kissing him. Kissing him and remembering the first time he entered my dreams. Kissing him and forgetting Christopher.

Even as the world fades, I realize this could all be in my head. But it doesn't really matter.

A branch breaks, sounding like a gunshot.

There's a tearing noise: stickers ripping fabric. I want to run. Except fleeing is pointless. I'll either crash into something sharp and rusty or continue through woods that won't thin out before Canada.

I remain motionless. Holding my breath is impossible. Smoke signals push past my lips. Beneath me, a rodent or some other sharp-toothed thing gnaws at the floorboard.

JACOB'S BODY

It's hard to hide in a car without doors.

I squeeze my eyes shut. When I open them, Jacob is gone.

The hand on my right arm provokes a scream so loud they probably hear it on campus.

Darlene doesn't flinch. She just stares at me, looking tired and annoyed. Looking, in fact, exactly like my mother did during the second half of my junior year.

"What the F is going on, Casey?"

I guess she wasn't as hard a sleeper as I thought.

CHAPTER TWENTY-FIVE

I stare at Darlene, at her violent violet ensemble, her mittens and wool cap matching her sweats. Biting my lip doesn't control the giggles. I crack up.

She's stone-faced. I hiccup hysterics, then gasp. "Oh my God, I'm about to be murdered by Barney!"

For a few seconds she just stares, unblinking. Then she raises her arms out in front of her. She lumbers beside the car and sings, *"One big happy family."*

My laughter fades as I extricate myself from the ruined Mustang. My legs ache from the cold. "How did you find me?" I stare at her, stretching. Finding yet another source of betrayal, I ask angrily, "Did Emily tell you about this place?"

"What? No way. Seriously, Case, you're nowhere near as…" She stumbles over a word, then says, "You're nowhere near as stealthy as you think you are."

"Stealthy? *Really.*"

"I heard you in the hallway, trying so hard to be quiet I knew you were up to something."

"Hard to believe you could hear anything over your snoring."

"I do *not* snore." I give her my best skeptical look. She ignores it. "Anyway, when I got downstairs you'd already disabled the alarm. I figured since you were using one of Sheila's old tricks you were back on the quest to find her. And here we are."

What did she see? From the woods, she probably didn't see anything. If I was kissing a ghost…

"Why were you in that car?"

"I was… thinking."

"What's going on, Case?"

I don't say anything. I want to tell her, I really do. I even struggle with the zipper on the knapsack but my fingers won't cooperate. Rubbing my hands together and blowing on them doesn't help. Trying to retrieve the map is harder than carving a pumpkin through a blanket. I finally give up, unsure of my next move.

"You found something at the cabin, didn't you? Why didn't you tell me?"

I think of three or four responses but don't say anything.

Darlene steps away from the Mustang, looks around. "You think she's here, don't you?"

"Maybe. I don't know."

"And your plan is what? Dig around at two a.m. with a crappy flashlight?"

"Hey, it's your flashlight."

"That's how I know it's crappy. Sucker shuts off at the worst times."

"Tell me about it." I go closer to the front of the Mustang and lean past the bumper. There's a shadow near the backhoe but I can't tell what it is, even with the flashlight.

"Well, you aren't going to find anything with hypo…hypo…"

"Hypothermia?"

She snaps her fingers. "Exactly."

"I'm fine, Mom." Darlene ignores my rudeness. I'm also not very convincing as my chattering teeth are probably scaring the wildlife.

"Listen, come back with me. I don't want you getting in trouble, hell even Sheila wouldn't want you to get in trouble. When it's light out, I'll help you look."

I still don't trust her but she's right. Except in daylight I'll be right back to where I started, having to figure out a way to get here without Darlene noticing. I'll be right back to doing this alone.

CHAPTER TWENTY-SIX

I hate that I can't trust Darlene. Because despite the gloom and cold, the walk back is better with her beside me. Just past the clearing, she peels off her purple gloves. "My hands are smaller than yours, but I don't care if you stretch them."

I work my fingers into them, feeling warmer immediately. "So, I went to the cabin you told me about. I found Jacob's file and when I looked through it there was a map. That clearing was circled."

"Oh-kay."

"Beside the circle, there was a note about Jacob. It was in Sheila's handwriting."

"You sure?"

"One hundred percent." I've read and re-read Sheila's journal. I could spot her cursive in a line-up, but I can't tell Darlene that. Instead, I tap her shoulder and say, "I'm pretty sure Sheila thinks Collins killed Jacob and his dad."

"That's nuts! Why would he kill anyone?"

"Collins didn't have much money, and Jacob's dad gave him a deal on the land. Maybe he changed his mind, or wouldn't give Collins everything he wanted. Then Sheila started asking questions and Collins got rid of her too."

"And what, Collins killed Amber for the same reason? And all the other teenagers that vanished?"

I shrug. "Maybe? I don't know. I'm still trying to figure it out."

She leans against a mess of thorns, pressing them out of the way so I can pass. As I do, she asks, "What if it isn't Collins, what if it's someone else at school?"

"Like who?"

"Well, that voice I told you I heard outside the cabin? That's not the first time I've been freaked out there."

"You really need a better mile marker."

"Tell me about it."

We're both silent for a minute, the glumping sound of our shoes slapping the moist ground the only noise. Then Darlene whispers, "It was right before Sheila left and I wasn't paying attention. When I raced around the cabin I almost ran into Keifer. He had a bunch of files and a couple of them fell to the ground. They were really old, I don't know why he needed them. I started to pick them up and... he smacked my hand away. I was so stunned I didn't say anything. He seemed really angry and nervous. I just turned and sprinted home."

"That's why you acted so weird the other day."

She nods. "Yeah. I mean, he's always creeped me out. He just seems like one of those old dudes who's always trying to look down your shirt when he thinks you won't notice."

"When have you ever worn shirts he could look down?"

Darlene laughs but all I can think about is what Emily said. I've never gotten a bad vibe from my cello teacher, but for all I know, he could be pervy to anyone he isn't teaching.

Except, wouldn't Sheila have noticed?

I stop, lean against a pine. "I just realized we aren't arguing the 'what,' only the 'who.'"

"Not saying I'm convinced. I love Sheila to death, but last year? She was always taking off, skipping curfew. I think she liked helping me, helping you. But I agree with Emily, she's the kind of girl to bolt without a note."

"Nice rhyme, Dorothy Parker."

"Thanks," she says with a snort. "Plus, if she had Jacob's file, maybe Collins or someone else caught her with it. Maybe it's not some scary movie, maybe they just asked her to leave because she'd stolen school property. Her being a star wasn't worth the trouble anymore."

"Maybe." I don't tell her that I've been thinking the same thing. Except in my version they do more than expel her. I don't say anything, because saying it out loud will make it real.

"The thing is, I believe Sheila *believes* it," Darlene says. "I believe you *believe* it."

"Which means what exactly?"

Darlene puts her hand on my arm and gently guides me onto the road. "You and she are pretty much the most amazing people I know. If you *both* believe the same thing, who am *I* to get in your way?"

"Wow. Thanks."

"I'm a bit bummed you didn't tell me about the map, though. Seriously, Casey, why didn't you ask me to come with?"

Darlene's hand is still on my wrist. I twist away from it, my voice cold and steady. "You didn't crash in Sheila's bed because of your dorm mate. You did it because Winter told you to."

I shift the flashlight in my hand and shine it on her. I can't tell if the pink of her face is from the cold or embarrassment. Denial develops in her eyes, but then she lowers her head. She's staring at her feet when she whispers, "Crap rolls downhill."

"What the heck does that mean?"

She lifts her head, stares at me. "You're the school's newest celebrity. Collins is helping Winter get into a grad program, so he's pushing her to make sure you don't trash another audition. She said I needed to start bunking with you. I told her you might need your space, and that's when she brought up my scholarship."

"*What?* The b—!" my curse interrupted when Darlene resumes walking.

I trail, trying to keep the light pointed a few steps ahead of us.

I can't see her face but she's breathing heavily as she says, "Hey, I don't blame her for wanting to get on with her life. And, really, I think she just wants you to be okay."

"Well, that video you shot of Winter really helped. I overheard Collins saying she was accepted."

"That's fantastic!"

I try to keep up—not just with her speed but with her emotions. I'm not sure how she can celebrate the achievements of someone who threatened her tuition. My lungs feel itchy. Talking is torture but I have more to say.

"If the headmaster really did kill Sheila, it's because he knew she found something out about him. Pretty much everything you tell Winter goes right back to Collins."

Through the trees, I can see a light or two from school. I stop walking. Maybe it's the exercise, maybe it's the borrowed gloves. I've gone from freezing to overheated. My breathing is ragged and ugly.

She grabs my shoulder. I'll never get used to how strong she is. Maybe it's just the cold air but tears are running down her face. "I've never said a word about you looking for Sheila. I won't. *Ever.* All I told Winter was that you were practicing every day and your audition piece sounded awesome. Heck, I even covered for you when you were off digging around the cabin and hanging with your boy."

"Good. Thank you." I try to slow my breathing. The wind picks up, bringing a scent like Christmas. "The thing is, I know you like Winter. I mean, I do too, but she and Collins… They're involved."

"What do you mean, 'involved'?"

"I heard them snogging."

"What? Speak English!"

"That is English." I laugh. "Making out, macking out, sharing spit…"

"Ewww, gross!"

"Yep. It was. But if you want to keep being Winter's lackey, then I'll be safer if you just leave me alone."

Before she can reply, I start climbing toward the converted house Jacob and his dad once called "Our New Place."

CHAPTER TWENTY-SEVEN

We pull our boots off on the porch and enter on sock-clad feet. I rearm the alarm while Darlene stands beside me. I'm on the bottom step when I glance back and notice she hasn't moved. I whisper, "What are you going to do, try to sneak back in without waking Morgan?"

She shrugs.

I wave her toward the stairs. "Come on, your things are up here."

We make it into my room without bumping into anyone. I close the door but leave the light off. My legs start to tighten, the muscles contracting painfully as they warm up. Beside me, Darlene is shivering. I drop my jacket onto the floor and peel off my mud-splattered jeans.

"I don't know how to say it other than to say it," Darlene says. "I won't tell Winter anything. I promise."

"Okay." My voice sounds flat. I dig under the bed for the packages, find the one I want and toss it to Darlene. "They're probably too big for you, but it's okay if you roll them up."

"Ha, ha." When she peels off her socks I realize they're soaked. She smiles gratefully as she tears open the package and pulls on the new wool socks.

I drag her comforter over to my bed, laying it across my sleeping bag before slipping beneath the sheets. Darlene hesitates beside her pillows. "Come on. If you don't join me, one of us might freeze to death."

She giggles as she grabs her pillows and gets in beside me. We fall asleep without another word.

CHAPTER TWENTY-EIGHT

It's after three and I have to use the bathroom. Rolling away from Darlene, I look back to make sure she's still asleep.

She isn't snoring, but she also doesn't stir as I leave the room.

I pause in the hallway. The light closest to my room is flickering. It wasn't doing that earlier. Then it goes out completely. I can't even see my door.

It's not a big deal, lights burn out. I take a deep breath and move toward it. Oak flooring groans beneath my feet.

The light comes back on.

Collins is leaning against the wall.

He's grinning. He hasn't shaved and bone-white stubble dots his chin.

Frigid air billows up from the stairway.

I won't let him into my room. I won't let him hurt Darlene.

I'd bargain or threaten or even scream but I can't. I'm unable to speak. The only thing escaping my mouth is a low hissing whine.

I back up and stare at him, refusing to blink. His eyes are the familiar bloodshot of hangovers. I keep one arm behind me, grasping for the banister. Before I reach it, my toes catch on a patch of unraveling carpet. There's a moment when I face a one-story tumble. At the last instant, my hand grasps the railing, jerking my arm all the way to my shoulder.

Collins finally moves, his speed zombie slow.

I descend.

He trails as I take the stairs sideways, one arm ready to defend myself, the other clutching the railing. He never bridges the gap; I don't stumble again. We continue in this weird waltz all the way to the first floor. That's when I finally turn around, moving toward the door. Collins is reflected in its glass, growing larger as he suddenly rushes toward me. I grab the knob, fumble with the lock, and he shoves me. *Hard.*

I slam on my side, roll and crash down the three steps to the sitting area. I rise on unsteady legs. He's already behind me. The headmaster wraps his arms around my chest and lifts me off the floor. I kick back, my heels smacking uselessly across his legs. He tosses me down the basement stairs. I land on one foot, halfway down the steps. Sharp pain shoots up my leg just before I go tumbling to the bottom and sprawl on the floor.

Cold from the concrete radiates through thin carpeting. Then I'm lifted by my waistband and set upright. It's agony to stand, let alone walk. Collins spreads one palm across the lowest part of my back and pushes me toward the music room.

When I try to twist away, his free hand tightens over my biceps.

My eyes water. I refuse to give him the satisfaction of hearing me whine, but I don't have any energy left for fighting.

It's over.

We pass the piano where Emily played, the sofa where Christopher waited. Inside the laundry room, twin washers are pushed against the dryers. Behind them, the exposed wall is two different colors; the middle section is lighter than the rest. It looks thin and shoddy.

At first, the noise is barely noticeable. It gets louder once we enter the room. I'm barely aware of the headmaster's forearm slipping across my neck; I'm too focused on the sound of fingernails frantically digging from the other side of the wall.

"Jacob?"

JACOB'S BODY

Collins strangles me, and my whole body shakes.

I start awake. Beside me, Darlene groans but doesn't shift. Her hip is pressed hard against my leg. It starts tingling as I extricate myself. This is the source of my pain, the reason it hurt so bad in my dream.

This time I leave my room for real.

CHAPTER TWENTY-NINE

The only thing I take is Darlene's flashlight. I'm still wearing just long underwear with the wool socks pulled up almost to my knees. The hallway is as dim and frightening as the one in my nightmare, absent the flickering light.

And Collins. As I head toward the stairs, I imagine him emerging from the shadows. Still, something about the remembered terror feels like trying to scare yourself as a kid, spending a winter afternoon pretending a monster is chasing you across the yard to the front door.

Back then, I knew I'd be safe and warm once I reached the other side.

I'm not sure what's waiting for me tonight and I'm not sure when I'll ever feel safe. At least I'm past calling myself crazy.

I forgot about the blueprint.

With all the escaping the dorm drama and trekking through dark woods and getting discovered by Darlene, I ignored the other clue. I ignored the paper I rescued from Sheila's things. I'm guessing this is why I had the dream, that for once I don't need a supernatural explanation.

It's maybe four a.m. Still dark, no hint of dawn or early risers. I've made it almost to the first floor when I stumble. My toe catches on a bit of raised carpet. I skip a step, then right myself. I'm so angry I could scream, pissed that I forgot this vital detail.

The rage grows darker when I put weight on my left ankle and real—not dream—pain blooms across my lower leg. Walking is almost impossible. I use the railing as a crutch, limping toward the sitting room. I bite my lip hard enough to bleed.

JACOB'S BODY

The music room is dark. I'm about to switch on the light atop the piano when I notice a glow coming from the laundry room. I creep past the instrument, head toward the open doorway.

I've reached the threshold when I notice the cello. I've only played the one here a few times. It feels weird in my hands but it's better than lugging my own from the music building every time I want to practice at the dorm. The cello is always in its case. Tonight the case is open, the cello resting by a chair. It faces a music stand. If I could see well enough to read the sheet music, I'm certain it would be for "Ave Maria."

My stomach feels like a dryer with a single damp washcloth rotating inside. Ignoring the unnerving sensation that real life is as threatening as my nightmares, I limp forward.

I try to be quiet. The music room is soundproof but someone lives just above the laundry room. The overhead light isn't very bright. I'm sure there's a dusty assortment of dead bugs waiting for me behind the machines. Worse, there's only enough room for me to shift the washer if I squat sideways with my butt sticking through the door. Something about not wearing shoes or pants makes me feel vulnerable. Every time I move, there's new bolt of pain. The washer squeaks when I grab it. By working slowly, pulling one end and then the other, I manage to move it several feet away from the wall.

My dream is verified. As I play the flashlight over the narrow gap, I notice several square feet where the paint is a lighter shade. Squeezing into the space, I manage enough leverage to move the other washer. Kneeling, I press my elbow against the lightest part of the wall. There's a satisfying pop. I stick my fingers in the small hole I made and start tearing. Hopefully the damage will be hidden when I replace the washers. Ignoring the pang of claustrophobia, I take a deep breath, squat down and continue peeling away chunks of wall.

I don't see him. But as I expand the space, I definitely *feel* him.

The next part is hard. I don't hesitate, knowing if I stop to think I'll stop completely. I push the flashlight through the hole I've just created. Then I press my cheek against the wall and look inside. It's the size of a coffin.

There's no body. If Jacob was killed or buried here, he was moved a long time ago. Probably around the time a hole was dug in the auto graveyard and other local kids started disappearing.

At either end of the space, plywood has been haphazardly nailed up. On the bottom, the flashlight illuminates a small patch the color of rust.

Blood?

I'm ready to call it a night when I see a flash of white. I press my face harder against the wall, one eye squinting into the crawlspace. The T-shirt is folded, almost hidden in the far corner. It's too white, too new looking to be 25 years old. Yet I have no doubt who it once belonged to. Maybe Jacob's killer was in a hurry, maybe he missed it. Maybe the spirit of Jacob's father kept it hidden, just so I could find it today.

Pressing my hips and shoulder against the wall and stretching my arm gives me almost enough reach. But I'm completely blind. Because of the angle, I can no longer look into the place where I think Jacob's body was once interred and I can't watch the laundry room. I close my eyes and grasp.

The end of the flashlight touches something soft. I press down, trapping it and dragging it toward me. There's a scraping sound.

JACOB'S BODY

My breath is heavy and hot, blowing back in my face from the wall. I keep pulling, my target slipping. I stretch further, get it a few inches more. I start to lean back a little, my eyes still shut, my ankle throbbing in time to my accelerated heartbeat.

A hand squeezes my shoulder and pulls me up, and I scream.

CHAPTER THIRTY

I cover the scream with a cough. Darlene is behind me, waving away bits of plaster. "Seriously?"

If I learn nothing else from tonight, it's that she's actually a light sleeper. Or I'm a clod.

I'm silent as I step back and hand her the light. She leans forward, takes a look. I don't know if she sees the T-shirt because before I can point it out, I hear piano music. Without a word, she pushes me gently out of the room and returns the washers to their original position with less effort than I'd exert lifting a purse.

I barely breathe as we enter the music room. After everything that's happened I expect to see Collins. Instead, Emily looks up as we pass, maybe not noticing I'm covered in drywall dust. But she doesn't say a word, her Berklee School of Music audition piece following us up the stairs.

It's almost dawn when Darlene and I enter the room. I know she wants to say something, but I ignore her, grabbing my shower caddy and towel. I don't expect her to still be in my room when I return, but she is.

"You think I'm a kid, don't you?"

I step back and turn on the light. She sits up in my bed, blinking. Her hair is messy and her eyes are watering. She actually looks about ten years old but I say as confidently as I can, "No, of course not."

"Or stupid. Maybe you think I'm stupid."

"Why? You're not the one who's breaking curfew and damaging school property." I grab a pair of sweats out of my dresser and go to the closet.

She shakes her head, looking as mad I've ever seen her. "I'm not joking! You're the only one who thinks Sheila is in trouble, the only one who thinks Collins did it. Now I find you tearing up a wall in the middle of the night."

"It was a feeling, that's all."

"Why don't you trust me enough to tell me the truth?"

"I do."

I open the closet door, hang up my towel, and start to pull on my sweats. Her voice is quiet from the other side. "No, you don't. I know a city girl like you might not notice, but that wall behind the washers? It was crappy. The kind of crappy you'd expect from—I don't know, a conductor who reads a book on do-it-yourself home repair?"

"I know."

"Because, hey, it's hard to find a subcontractor for sealing up a dead teen... , teen..." And then she starts bawling.

I walk around the door and pull her to me. Despite being so powerful, she's still small and, yeah, she seems like a little girl. But I know she isn't. Darlene gets a few tissues from my nightstand, wipes her eyes. "Are you going to be honest with me?"

"I didn't lie exactly. I just didn't tell you everything."

She grimaces. "My mom's Catholic. That's what she'd call 'a sin of omission.'" She pulls away from me. "How did you know to look there? It wasn't on a map."

"It was on a blueprint."

I go to my knapsack, grateful I don't have to come clean about the ghosts of Jacob, his dad, Amber. That I don't need to count on Darlene's romantic imagination. I spread the blueprint out on the bed and tap the red square. "While my boy was talking to Collins about European EDM stars, I was digging around the

Headmaster's Residence. There's this storeroom where I found all of Sheila's stuff. Looked sad and abandoned."

"Wow."

"Yeah. Anyway, I found this, and since my little forest adventure didn't pan out, I went with Plan B."

Darlene looks at it for about ten seconds before she says, "That's not the laundry room."

"What are you talking about?" I squeeze beside her and point to the paper. "There's the sitting area, the music room, the laundry room..."

She takes my finger and moves it a quarter inch. "*That's* the laundry room—that narrow rectangle. The space you were tapping is where you were digging. The red square is farther back—with not one but two walls between it and the washers. I'm guessing the second one is a bit sturdier. So, unless you can clear out the dorm and rent some power tools..."

"Great! *Perfect night.*" I move away from her and stretch, grateful that at least my ankle feels a little better. "Did you see anything through the hole I made?"

She shakes her head. "Dust mainly. Maybe bloodstains but..."

"There was a T-shirt. I was trying to get it out when you interrupted me."

"You think it's a clue? What does a T-shirt have to do with anything?"

Darn. I really thought I could get away with not telling her everything. *Nice job.*

"Casey?"

"Every time I see Jacob, he's wearing a white T-shirt. That's why I asked you about Sheila's boyfriends a week ago, when I said he didn't dress for the weather."

"What are you talking about? 'Every time you see Jacob?' What does that mean?"

"I've seen him. I've seen Jacob, and his dad and … the dead girls. Like I'm starring in my own scary movie where I either wind up dead or in the loony bin."

Darlene pauses. She wipes her nose with a tissue, looking deep in thought. "I don't think you're crazy. Your dad died, right?"

"Are you saying grief is making me hallucinate?"

"No. Not at all. Sheila was supposed to live with her grandmother but she got real sick. She didn't want to go with her parents to China and they wouldn't let her stay by herself in New York. That's why she came here."

"Sheila must really hate her parents."

"Or China," she says with a giggle. Then, more serious, she adds, "Her grandmother died last spring."

"Okay."

"My point is maybe you and she are more connected to Jacob and the rest. Because you both lost someone recently."

"Makes as much sense as anything else." I fold up the blueprint and return it to my knapsack. "I need to get that shirt, but it's going to be impossible before the music room clears out at curfew. Plus, well, there's the whole dilemma of getting through two walls without Winter noticing. So, it looks like I'm headed back to that clearing where you found me. I really think it could lead me to Sheila."

"I'm going to help. I'll cover for you with Winter and everything. But it's barely light, you've barely slept, and if you leave now you're more likely to break your leg than save someone. You need sleep. We both do."

I'm too tired to argue, and her comment about a broken leg is too close to real life and my nightmare.

So, I slip in beside her, my hair still wet, the smell of body wash and shampoo finally erasing the smell of blood that's been in my nostrils for what seems like days. I'm asleep the moment my head hits the pillow.

CHAPTER THIRTY-ONE

I wake up facing the closet. The door is still ajar. Open closet doors are like a lot of things that only seem scary in the dark.

Sun streams through the blinds. I know I've slept for a while, beautiful dreamless sleep. Darlene is pressed against my back, her left arm draped over my side. Her hand is an inch from my boob.

Something about it seems like the morning after, like a random hook-up or a friend with unexpected benefits. Those are pretty much the only messes I've avoided this year.

I try to shift. She spoons closer.

For a few minutes, I just lie there. I feel weird and uncomfortable, yet I'm oddly grateful. I've woken up beside a warm body two mornings in a row.

I stretch my arms.

"Five more minutes, Mom."

"I wasn't sure if you were awake."

"Mmmhmm. Just not ready to deal with cold floor and cold hall."

"I know." I'd hoped to be up when the other kids were at breakfast. It feels closer to brunch. "Darlene?"

"Yeah."

"It's okay if you think I'm nuts."

She lifts her arm and rubs my shoulder before sitting up. I look back at her. With her messy hair and round face, she resembles one of those little girls on birthday cards that grandmothers buy. "I already told you. I don't think you're nuts."

"It's cool if you do. But I just want you to know, despite everything, I'm not going to screw up my Conservatory audition. No matter what happens, Sheila wouldn't want that."

"I believe you."

"If Sheila is in trouble and I don't do anything, I'll never forgive myself."

"I know. I feel the same way. But I thought of something while you were snoring."

"I don't snore," I complain, smiling a little.

"Let's say you're right, right about *everything*."

I sit up, so that we are both beside each other with our legs beneath warm covers. "Okay, let's say I'm right. Which usually feels better than this, by the way."

"If you're right, Collins isn't *just* lying to us. He's lying to Sheila's *parents* too."

"Maybe. But what if he only *said* he was talking to them. They're somewhere like here, no cell, no web, yeah?"

"Yeah."

"So, he could get away with it until winter break. Maybe longer, if she'd planned on staying on campus for the holidays."

"Yeah, but it's moronic. If Collins killed her, and he's lying about where she is, eventually someone is going to figure it out."

I push hair off my face even as I realize something important. "He's a musician, Darlene."

"What's that got to do with it?"

"He's *improvising*. He didn't know what he was going to play until he had to play it. Collins probably felt more like a conductor with Jacob and his dad. He planned it well enough to not get caught. But Sheila? Sheila wasn't planned. She said the wrong thing at the wrong time and she wound up like Amber Perkins."

Darlene rubs her hands for a moment, staring at her ragged nails. She looks up at me, her voice barely audible when she says,

"You really think Sheila's dead."

I tap her arm and shake my head when she finally looks at me. "No. I *don't*. We have time. Not much but…" I give her arm a squeeze. "It's why I was willing to catch cold last night."

"How do you know for sure Sheila's okay?"

"You know Sherman, at Elba's?"

"Sure. He keeps me in art books and trashy novels."

"Well, he and I talked after I was at the newspaper. He told me his suspicions, about Collins and Jacob. But he also told me something he overheard the cops saying after Amber's body was found."

"What's that?"

"She was missing for two weeks but she was killed right before they found her."

"So, if Sheila was taken by the same person who took Amber…"

"Then she's probably still alive. But if I don't find her, before I leave for my audition, she'll be murdered right around the time I'm ripping through Joplin at The Conservatory."

CHAPTER THIRTY-TWO

I convince Darlene to stay behind. I hate trekking to the clearing by myself again. But I'm *not* doing this alone. She's helping me. Her job is to stay in my room. When Winter knocks, as I know she will, Darlene will tell her I'm still sleeping, that we were up watching movies all night.

I even made a fake me with pillows.

Darlene insisted on loading me with provisions. I'll have to be pretty hungry before I try the low-carb crackers, but I'm grateful for the water and almonds.

Hopefully, I can discover whatever there is to be discovered before it gets too late. Because I need to be in my practice room before Collins starts pressuring Winter even more than he already is.

Instead of cutting through the woods to the road, I decide to cross campus. Later, I'll wonder if that one decision was why everything went bad in a hurry.

It's warm for November, but overcast. With my new thermies and borrowed gloves, I feel prepared for anything. Darlene even found new batteries for the flashlight.

I pass through The Academy's far gate and walk parallel to the road. The pink bandanna seems way too easy to spot, now that I know it's there. Something about it makes me feel uneasy, enough that I almost remove it. I don't, but as I push onto the small path, I worry it will make me easier to follow.

In the daylight, I avoid the worst of the sticker bushes. Still, by the time I reach the clearing my ankle is screaming and I need to lean against a tree. The sun is obscured by clouds and diffused by pines. Wrecked machinery resembles hungry carnivores, the rusted blades ready to rip me apart.

I enter the aisle. Shadows mask the edges of objects. I'm claustrophobic in their midst.

Why did Jacob appear to me? Is Sheila our only real connection? Or is there something deeper, something primal? Am I drawn to him because he can answer all my questions or am I falling for a ghost?

The Mustang is empty. Despite everything, this makes me more than a little sad.

It's not easy to maneuver around. The rear is pressed against a tractor with part of the back fender flush against an enormous tire. The front bumper is hard by the backhoe's tracks, which look like something from a tiny tank. In daylight, I realize the machine is newer than the others, but still coated in grime and cobwebs.

I can't handle the front seats. Squeezing past the steering wheel is too scary. What if Jacob suddenly appears as I occupy his spot? What would *that* feel like? I climb into the back. Sliding across the wrecked leather, a spring snags the pocket of my jeans. I feel fabric tear as I squirm away. "Dammit!"

My voice is weak and unfamiliar.

I am weak and unfamiliar.

I set my knapsack down and remove the flashlight. Then I step through the gap where the door would be. I see what I'm looking for almost immediately. I dreamed it in the library, just like the car. It's a few feet from the front tire. Dirt piled beside it leads right to the backhoe—probably the only thing that works in this weird junkyard. Propped against it are a shovel and a large sheet of plywood.

It isn't a hole. It's a trench.

Moving closer, I bend forward. It's about four feet wide and extends at least 15 feet, mostly hidden beneath slats of wood and packed soil. It's at least two feet deeper than I am tall. The sides are packed tight and slick like clay. I get dizzy peering over the edge.

The trench is empty.

I feel bereft. Part of me believed that if the hole existed the same way the Mustang existed, then Sheila would be here and I could save her.

Instead, I'm going to have to tell Darlene that I found something that could be a clue. Or it could be intended for the interment of oil cans and car parts.

I'm turning when something sparkles in the dim light. The object is a couple of feet down the trench wall. I turn on the flashlight and play its beam across the hole. The light reveals a small handprint, preserved like a fossil. It looks like it was left by a petite girl, not the boy who shared the broken car with me.

Getting on my knees like I'm praying, I peel off the gloves and yank.

It's a piece of jewelry, and I recognize it immediately. Sheila's bracelet, the one she was wearing the day we met. I'd asked her about it. She told me it was braided from silk and the violin strings from the first instrument she ever played.

Sheila left her bracelet for me to find. And I finally have proof. She's been here. For all I know, she's been here the whole time.

I'm considering this as I stand. I'm looking forward to getting back, to showing my discovery to Darlene.

JACOB'S BODY

Two hands smack against my shoulders. My arms pinwheel as I skid down the side of the hole. The flashlight spins ahead of me, plopping into the soft ground just before I land beside it. The impact jolts my sprained ankle and travels up my spine.

I raise my eyes toward the surface and scream loud enough to hurt my own ears. Collins drops the plywood across the hole. Dirt falls in shovelfuls over the wood.

CHAPTER THIRTY-THREE

Screaming is pointless. No one is around. Even better, I managed to swallow some dirt. Which means my mouth now tastes like a repair shop's concrete floor. I ache for Darlene's parting gift, the food and water. Without thinking about it, I feel around for my knapsack.

It's still in the Mustang.

My fingers are going numb. I left the gloves beside the hole. So, if I don't figure a way out of this, frostbite is going to start claiming body parts. Shoving my hands between my thighs, I inhale deeply, wondering how many more breaths I have left.

Sheila could be a few feet or a few thousand miles away. She's probably dead.

She might have had days to live. My expedition has probably shortened that. If Collins hasn't already killed her, he will soon.

If no one finds me, *no one will even know why I disappeared.* My mom, my boyfriend, Keifer—everyone will just assume broken little Casey cracked under the pressure. They'll figure I skipped out on school, on the audition. They'll look for me for a bit, sure. But I can see them assuming I just caught a bus or decided to hitchhike.

I'll be written off by most as just another disappeared runaway. Which means I managed to fail both Sheila *and* my talent. And my dad.

Only Collins knows the truth. This time, he probably won't leave my body in some field like he did with Amber. Old dirt and new snow could conceal this hole for months. Maybe in the spring some bored couple will stroll right over me without knowing I'm here.

As a hot tear meanders down my cheek, I sense a different hole—a gap in my theory. I'm too hungry, cold, and scared to figure out what it is.

A scream grows. I clamp my teeth shut.

There's no point.

I stretch my legs and stand up. My ankle hurts even worse than it did last night. I think about Amber and wonder if my last moments will be like hers. I think about the other missing girls.

All of us in a final communion of death.

Despite the board and dirt blocking the entrance, it's not completely dark. There's a shadow halfway up, something unearthed as I fell. I stretch my arms and grab it. It's thick and hard, a root or some piece of machinery. It's difficult to tell what it is because I've lost almost all feeling in my fingers.

The stick-like thing holds fast when I pull, so I dig my toes in and begin hoisting myself up. With a bit of luck and leverage I can get out of here.

There's a brief intoxicating moment when I sense victory, when I anticipate escaping and sending our homicidal headmaster to prison.

When I believe I really will save Sheila.

Then the root comes lose from the chilled earth. I fall backward, smacking my butt hard. I yell, more from rage and defeat than fear.

I feel around for the flashlight. My handhold fell nearby but it takes a moment of playing the light across the trench before I see it. My stomach drops as I realize that it isn't a root.

It's a bone.

I took anatomy last year. It looks human—I think it's a femur.

There are other explanations but if it really belonged to a person then I know something else. It's something I can feel in my own bones.

I've found Jacob's body.

JACOB'S BODY

CODA

    I'm screaming again. I'm ten feet underground and in the middle of nowhere. I scream until my throat aches and I'm gasping for breath. Looking up, I'm rewarded with new information.

    It's snowing.

    Flakes flow through gaps around the plywood, drifting down and settling on exposed skin. They melt on my cheeks, my eyelashes, my hands. I'm too numb to feel anything.

    <u>*Too numb*</u>*.*

    And tired. So tired.

    The day is dying and I'm fading along with it.

    Then there is light. Bright as the sun, impossible to look at. I no longer need the flashlight to see my hands, my feet. The cramped quarters expand, the ground stretches outward as the slick clay walls move away, fading into the distance and replaced by endless space.

    He emerges from the light. Even in silhouette I recognize him immediately.

    His hair is shaggy, the way it gets when he's been touring. He's dressed as he was for the last performance he ever gave. His tuxedo is freshly pressed. On stage he wore a tie, but now his collar is open and bare. It's how he must have looked speeding home after the concert, speeding toward me.

    He's finally made it.

    He's tall and I'm still sitting on the ground. Peering up, I feel about eight years old. I have a powerful memory of my first snow day, holding his hand and watching white flakes form new shapes over parked cars and twinkling trees. Staying home from school

THE ACADEMY

could have been an excuse for more cello practice. Instead, we spend the day playing on the usually busy streets. We have a snowball fight. He pulls me on a toboggan.

Afterward, Mom makes us hot chocolate.

It was a lifetime ago.

When I finally stand, my legs are no longer shaky. When I put weight on my ankle, it not longer throbs. I move toward him, passing the point where the walls should stop me. As I slide closer to my father, I have one final thought.

This isn't a hole. This isn't a trench.

It's a grave.

THE END

ACKNOWLEDGMENTS

Writing is sometimes lonely but no one truly writes a book alone. Anytime you pick up a book, trust that there are legions of people behind its publication.

First, I want to thank the many teachers, professors and editors who mentored me over the years. Special thanks to Louella Nelson and the University of California, Irvine, Advanced Novel Writing Workshop. Your emphasis on form but not formula was a true blessing as was the feedback from classmates.

I want to thank Jenny Bent and her colleagues at The Bent Agency who took *The Academy* through several rounds of notes and revisions. I also want to thank Spencer Robinson of Art/Work Entertainment. Your course on writing TV pilots and my picturing *The Academy* as a TV series really helped me overcome some early issues with plot while deepening the mystery.

I've been blessed to have a number of supportive, encouraging women in my life. They helped me keep the faith despite the normal rejections and dark times that all writers must confront. I especially want to thank Karen Paul, Kimberly Davis, and Lora Noesen.

I want to thank Sue Wilkins for your amazing work editing this trilogy. Your insights and encouragement were true gifts. You had a light touch, but a significant one.

Thank you to Ed Morgan for an amazing job with the covers. You made my imagination a reality.

Thanks to the many Wattpad readers who responded to early drafts of this story.

Last but by no means least, thank you to Phil Comer who recognized some early potential in a standalone novel and encouraged me to transform it into a trilogy. You stood by this project during the most challenging period of our lives. This book would not exist without your extraordinary efforts.

John Bankston

Photo by Joe Lyman, Huntington Beach, California, September 2022.